THE
D'EVIL
DIARIES

To my parents, for always being there, come hell or high water.
And to all the kids who worry about being different. Remember:
heroes are never the same as everyone else.

ORCHARD BOOKS
338 Euston Road, London NW1 3BH
Orchard Books Australia
Level 17/207 Kent Street, Sydney, NSW 2000

First published in the UK in 2015 by Orchard Books

ISBN 978 1 40833 576 5

Text © Natasha Ellis 2015
Illustrations by Dave Shephard © Orchard Books 2015

The right of Natasha Ellis to be identified as the author of this work has been
asserted by her in accordance with the Copyright, Designs and Patents Act, 1988.

A CIP catalogue record for this book is available from the British Library.

1 3 5 7 9 10 8 6 4 2

Printed and bound by CPI Group (UK) Ltd, Croydon, CR0 4YY

Orchard Books is an imprint of Hachette Children's Group and published by
The Watts Publishing Group Limited, an Hachette UK company.

www.hachette.co.uk

THE
D'EVIL
DIARIES

ABANDON HOPE ALL
YE WHO ENTER
HERE

TATUM FLYNN

ORCHARD

Contents

'Some saye in sporte, and thinke in earnest:
The devill is not so blacke as he is painted.'

Sir Thomas More, Dialogue of Comfort, 1553

1

What's the Plural of Nemesis, Anyway?

HIGH ABOVE THE cavernous glass roof of The Poison Gardens, the crimson skies of Pandemonium swirled lazily over the city. Inside the greenhouse, the spiked black branches of the Nemesis Tree swooped and darted like kraken tentacles searching for ships. The sap oozing from the Tree's trunk was bright yellow and smelled uncannily of mouldy trainers. Any creature unlucky enough to get too close would be swept up before being slowly crushed to death.

I knew all this because I was hanging upside down from the treetop.

And the branches round my ankles were really starting to pinch.

A small crowd had gathered below. They gaped up at me, open-mouthed. In the middle stood Mr Frumble, my biology teacher. Mr Frumble was a rotund, jolly-looking demon with blue horns, blue skin, and a blue bowtie. That

jolliness did not extend to his personality.

'Jinx D'Evil, you calamitous, cack-handed carbuncle! How the devil did you get up there?' he thundered.

It's hard to shrug when you're upside-down. 'Bad luck?' I mumbled, trying not to dribble onto my horns.

I never did have much luck on field trips.

That morning, before we'd trooped off the school bus, Frumble had pointed threateningly at us. 'Don't touch anything unless I say so, and whatever you do, don't go near the Nemesis Tree. It's the last of its kind in Hell and a protected species. Also, it'll eat you for breakfast.'

The busload of red-skinned, black-winged twelve-year-olds muttered vaguely back at him.

'But in case of emergency, you all have the antidotes you made last week, right?'

We dutifully waved the vials of liquid we'd prepared in the previous lesson. My eyes grew wide. Oh, brimstone. *Purple*. They were all purple. Mine, on the other hand, was a sludgy brown. Oh well, it wasn't likely I'd have to use it.

Frumble clanked open the bus door. 'OK, follow me. I think you'll find The Poison Gardens both educational and exciting.'

I looked down past my dangling arms. Frumble's eyes were nearly popping out of his blue face. I don't think he'd expected quite this level of excitement.

By this point my whole class was there, every tiny horned figure hollering and jeering up at me. I'd never exactly been popular. Two voices cackled louder than the rest – Benny and Arael, the demons who'd thought it would be funny to trip me just as we were walking past the Tree. The Tree was not my only nemesis. I tried to dribble in their general direction.

'Waterfalls, Jinx,' yelled Arael. 'Think waterfalls. And

lakes, and dripping showers, and splashing waves.'

Oh, brilliant. Now I needed to pee. Just when I thought things couldn't get any worse.

Another spiked Nemesis branch snaked towards me.

That was worse.

Did I mention I hate field trips?

My eyes were watering and my head felt like it was about to explode. A lone teardrop ran down my brow and plopped to the ground.

'Aw, crying for Daddy, are we?' sneered Benny.

I decided if I fell to my death I would aim for him.

'Use the antidote, D'Evil!' shouted up an increasingly panicked-looking Frumble.

The antidote. Yep. Right. The antidote which was meant to be swallowed if you were bitten by a grabbersnutch plant, or spiked by a verlinder petal. Not as a weapon against something which could actually pick you up and eat you.

But since no one seemed to be coming to my rescue with a chainsaw, I didn't have much choice.

I reached up into my – thankfully zipped – jacket pocket, grabbed the vial and yanked the lid off. An evil smell wafted out. Ugh. Well, maybe it would startle the Tree enough for it to loosen its grip on my ankles. I took a deep breath and flung the brown mixture into the nearest branches.

Unsurprisingly, nothing happened.

Brilliant. Now what?

The Tree shrieked.

OK, that was surprising.

It shrieked again, and the branches holding me shook. Then, before my eyes, the Nemesis Tree began to change. Spikes shrivelled and dropped off, and the colour of the bark turned from inky black to healthy brown.

Then little pink flowers burst out everywhere.

'What in Lucifer's name...?' squawked Mr Frumble.

The branches holding me were suddenly smooth and flowery, and smelling of...bubblegum?

Oh no. I'd really done it this time. The Nemesis was no longer a monstrous bringer of death. I'd turned the most evil tree in Hell *Good*.

But who cared? I was saved! I would live to see my thirteenth birthday after all. A broad grin spread across my face. I was so relieved I forgot I was still fifty feet up in the air.

Until the tree, which was now humming gently to itself, dropped me.

Uh oh. Flying was so not my strong suit. I flapped my wings frantically, rose a foot into the air, then went into a tailspin and whirled down, and down...and landed with a crunch.

11

On top of a blue-skinned, blue-horned demon wearing a bowtie.

'D'Evil!' he bellowed. 'I am going to skin you and make you into a handbag! A handbag, do you hear me?'

So much for being happy to be alive.

# 2

Be Careful
What You Wish For

THE SECOND WORST feeling in the world is realising you've done something mammothly, brontosaurusly stupid. The absolute worst? Waiting to find out exactly how much trouble your stupid has landed you in.

And after getting home I'd been waiting in my attic bedroom, with no one but the spikemoths huddled in the rafters for company, for six long, agonising hours. I'd done restless pacing and tortured gazing-out-of-the-window, and was onto desperately-wondering-how-to-mail-yourself-to-Earth, when finally I heard it.

A knock at the door.

Not just any knock: an *important-sounding* knock. My heart sank so far into my boots I could've used it as a pair of nice comfortable insoles. This was it, then. I took a deep breath and yanked the door open quickly to get the pain over with.

A wizened grey demon stood outside, spindly wings still

fluttering like he'd arrived in a hurry. He fixed me with glowing red eyes. 'Lucifer, Prince of Darkness, Enemy of Righteousness, Lord of the Flies, summons you. Follow me and I shall take you to my master. Refuse, and the consequences—'

'Yes, yes, I get it,' I interrupted, rolling my eyes. 'You could just say my dad wants to see me.'

The messenger demon blinked at me. There was an awkward silence. 'Do you refuse to follow me, Jinx D'Evil?' he said finally.

I sighed. 'Of course not.' Who dares deny the Devil?

I stuck my hands in my pockets and trudged off to meet my doom.

My problem is I'm a lousy demon. I'm just terrible at being terrible. And a fundamental failure to be evil is not something that's supposed to happen to Lucifer's youngest son. It's not like I don't try. I really do. But things always seem to backfire when I'm around – and the next thing you know there's been a gigantic explosion of Goodness and everyone's turning pointy tail and running for cover.

The grey demon ushered me through the echoing stairwells and corridors of the palace, until we came to the regal, black marble hallway which led to Dad's study. Gold-framed paintings filled with war and gore covered the walls, and carved busts of illustrious demons sneered down at me from their plinths. The messenger slipped inside and left me to contemplate my own total lack of illustriousness.

I kicked the wall in frustration. Bad idea. I caught the toe of my trainer in a crack in the marble, hopped about on one leg like a drunken flamingo, then lost my balance and landed with a crash. As I lay sprawled on the hard stone floor, I considered the possibility this was not my day. Or year.

I got up with as much dignity as I could muster, brushed the dust off my trousers and crept closer to the vast double doors that stood between me and certain death. They were made of heavy black wood, every inch carved into twisting snakes, cackling gargoyles and winged demons. As I leant forward to eavesdrop, a shiny black cobra flared up and hissed at me. I smacked it on the nose and peered through the keyhole into the study.

Lucifer was sulking. He sank deeper into his armchair, listlessly tapping cigar ash into the mouth of a quivering glutton kneeling at his feet. I'd chosen a bad week to get in trouble. Takings were down throughout Hell, and my mum Persephone's calming influence was nowhere to be found, since she was off on holiday again. Dad was staring at a square piece of paper in his huge red hand.

My report card. I was toast.

He glanced up. 'All right, send him in.'

The messenger demon nodded and came towards the doors. I backed away hurriedly as they swung open.

He cleared his throat. 'Lucifer, Prince of...'

I slid past the continuing litany of titles and shut the doors behind me before I lost my nerve. 'Dad, I—'

'Quiet, boy!' he roared, his black eyes flashing red with anger.

I quieted. Dad might've had the same deep red skin,

16

dark hair and curling horns as me, but he was a solid eight foot tall and built like a weight-lifting buffalo. As a scrawny twelve-year-old who couldn't lift much more than a bag of schoolbooks, I was in no position to argue. He rose and advanced on me like a bear about to devour its young. Which there were rumours he'd actually done to my half-brother Fremiel. I backed away, quaking, and in a wild moment of panic, gave him puppy eyes, hoping the baby blues I'd inherited from Mum might calm him down. He waved the report card at me and snarled. So much for that plan.

'What kind of half-term report do you call this, hmm? I wouldn't mind if you failed because you were playing truant, or chasing girls, or trying to set fire to your teacher with a flamethrower. Boys will be boys! But to...' He held up the piece of paper. 'To "pay very careful attention, obey all your teachers, and work extremely hard"! It's inexcusable. What do you have to say for yourself?'

I became very interested in my feet. 'I tried, Dad,' I mumbled into my chin. 'Honestly. That thing with the Nemesis Tree was an accident, I didn't mean to—'

'Ah, the Nemesis. One of Hell's most infamous landmarks, for thousands of years,' he said slowly, before exploding in a rage. 'Two minutes in your vicinity and it's

17

gone from a bloodthirsty venomous creature to a pink flowery plant that smells of bubblegum! *Bubblegum!* How can you get things so wrong, Jinx?'

'I'm sorry, Dad. I'll try harder.'

'Well, I can't have a son of mine failing his Evil Levels, it's an embarrassment. I'm sending you for private tuition with a master of the dark arts: Edward Teach, better known as Blackbeard, the most dastardly pirate ever to sail the seven seas.'

Gah. That's what I got for the whole desperately-wondering-how-to-mail-yourself-to-Earth thing. Be careful what you wish for.

'When?'

'Tomorrow. You'd better get this right, Jinx, or there will be consequences. Very serious consequences, do you understand?'

I gulped and nodded.

'Now get out of my sight, I've got sixteen species to make extinct by lunchtime, and I need to work on my golf swing.' He turned his back on me.

I left his study and shuffled off down the hall. I tried so hard to be evil, but bad luck just seemed to follow me around like a lovesick zombie. A lovesick zombie who'd broken a mirror and walked under a ladder. Was it my fault

Benny and Arael had shoved me into the waiting tentacles of the tree? Was it my fault the antidote hadn't worked properly? I was only a third year, not some kind of science genius. I sighed. All I wanted to do was make Dad proud, like my big brother Dantalion had done, driving his chariot straight through the ozone layer and leaving a gaping hole. Or my sister Morgana, inventor of homework, paper cuts, and a range of bikes that automatically fell over on gravel.

At least it meant I'd get out of school for a while. I wasn't a huge fan of school. Or rather, school wasn't a huge fan of me. Surprisingly, being a disaster magnet wasn't the best way to win friends and influence demons. No one wanted to go near the weirdo who ended up with a rainbow instead of napalm in Chemistry, or the dunce who accidentally emailed half of Europe kitten GIFs instead of a killer virus in ICT. Not to mention my total lack of prowess at flying, which ruled me out of ever winning back any cool points playing Air Hockey. As a result, I didn't have a single friend there. I could hardly blame them; they were scared my horrible luck would rub off on them.

I wished it was winter. Winter meant Mum back home. *She* never yelled at me or called me a poor excuse for a demon. True, that might've been because she'd missed several of my most spectacular failures while she was busy applying suntan lotion in Greece. Or simply because she was a goddess. Literally. But I'd have taken cheerful denial any time.

I stopped halfway up the long, winding staircase to catch my breath, and peered out of an arrow slit. The family castle, Darkangel Palace, was so big there were dozens of rooms I'd never even been in. Perched on a rocky outcrop surrounded by a moat of fire, its gleaming black turrets looked out over the looming nothingness of the Great Abyss to the north, and the twisted red skyscrapers of Pandemonium and frozen wastelands of Outer Hell to the south. It was a lovely view.

When I reached my bedroom I slammed the door behind me. An alarmed snuffling sound came from the ceiling.

'Hmph, woke me up,' said Loiter, poking his furry head out of a hammock hanging from the rafters.

'I always wake you up when I come in, because you're always asleep.'

He tilted his head to one side. 'You make a good point.'

Loiter was a three-toed sloth, which wasn't surprising since he was the Patron Demon of Sloth, or Laziness. There was a Patron Demon for each of the Seven Deadly Sins, but Loiter avoided most of his colleagues as much as possible, because, as he often complained, 'They're so *ambitious.*

Always running around, trying to tempt humans into sin. Makes me tired just looking at them.' Since I was useless at being evil, and Loiter generally couldn't be bothered to be, we got on pretty well.

He scratched his belly. 'Ah well, refill my glass, would you? There's a good chap.'

On top of a bookcase stood a margarita glass so large, it wouldn't have looked amiss if a few goldfish had been swimming in it. The glass was connected to a very long straw, which snaked all the way up to the hammock. I peered into the fridge and located a bottle of bright green liquid that looked like it could strip paint off a lamppost. I emptied it into the glass and watched the liquid slurp upwards. Loiter smacked his lips, then rootled around in his fur, brought out a pack of cigarettes, and lit one.

'Ahhh, that's better. Cigarettes were my greatest invention, you know. Makes people feel like they're doing something even if they're only lounging in an armchair.'

'Killed a lot of humans too,' I added.

'Yes, your father was thrilled about that. Figure after such a resounding success I'm due a wee sabbatical for a few centuries.' He blew a smoke ring at the ceiling. 'So, where have you been? Getting into trouble again?'

I sat down on the bed and sighed dramatically. 'It's that

21

whole thing with the Nemesis Tree. Dad's really mad at me. He's sending me away to stay with Blackbeard.'

'Well, that doesn't sound so bad, I hear Tortuga's quite nice this time of year. Come on, cheer up, I'll beat you at Mario Kart if you like.'

'You got a bootleg Earth copy?' The Hellish version was called Killer Kannibal Kart and gave me nightmares.

'Yup, got it on the white market.' He dropped down to the floor and picked up a controller. 'Ready to lose horribly?'

I sat down beside him with a smirk. Maybe my only friend was a several-thousand-year-old sloth, but he always managed to cheer me up. I picked up a controller and revved up my engine. 'You wish.'

Early the next morning, I hiked my backpack up on my shoulder and made my way down the steep staircase that led to The Waiting Room, deep in the bowels of Darkangel Palace. I pushed open the creaky door and gagged, as usual, at the rotten-egg stench of brimstone. Dozens of pale fiends – temptation demons who spent most of their time on Earth – lined the wooden benches of the vaulted stone room, bickering with one another while they filled in forms to allow them passage to their destinations.

Demons came in all shapes and colours: tiger-headed, dragon-bodied, blue- and purple-tinged, although the majority were red-skinned and pointy-tailed like me. But fiends gave me the creeps a little, because their skin was near translucent, and you could see the blue blood pumping through their veins. Plus they *always* stank of brimstone.

I sighed, took a form from a table and set to work. Hellish visas were really complicated.

Twenty minutes later, shaking my sore hand, I joined the long queue snaking up to the central iron door which led to Earth. Above it, two giant brass wheels clanked and shuddered as fiends entered and exited.

When I reached the front, a monstrously fat green demon called Horslath took my form. 'Jinx D'Evil? To Tortuga? In the year 1717?'

I nodded three times.

Horslath twitched his horns and squinted at the piece of paper. 'Your handwriting is appalling, young man. Reason for visit?'

'Sorry. Private tuition.'

'With Blackbeard, I expect? Right ho.' He took a step back and snapped his fingers at the two uniformed wheel-masters behind him.

They took hold of a lever each, and pressed down hard.

The brass wheel on the left turned slowly, past Beijing and Salem and somewhere called Little Piggleswick, then clicked to a stop at Tortuga. The one on the right followed suit, spinning through the centuries until it arrived with a jolt at 1717.

I took a deep breath. Eighteenth-century Caribbean, here I came. I made a promise to myself: when I got there, I would be the evilest demon the world had ever seen. Blackbeard himself would quake at my villainy. I would get it right this time, whatever it took.

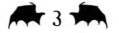 3

The Problem With Pirates

THE ISLAND OF Tortuga was a spoonful of golden sand dropped into the turquoise waters of the Caribbean Sea like sugar in a giant's teacup. Sunshine sparkled, birds trilled, and cloudless blue skies shimmered high above.

Basically, it was a demon's worst nightmare.

Blackbeard strode down the gangplank to meet me as I stood on the harbour, squinting and sweating and wishing I'd brought shades. A dark coat lined in red strained over his broad shoulders and his long black beard was tied into plaits and woven with filthy ribbons. He gave me a toothless grin. 'Pleased to meetcha, m'lad! Come aboard, come aboard.'

What did you say to an infamous, bloodthirsty pirate who ruled the waves with a fist of iron? I gulped. 'Hello, Mr Blackbeard.'

He laughed. 'Call me Ed, lad, call me Ed.'

Ed. Alrighty then. Maybe this wasn't going to be so bad after all.

The next morning, the *Queen Anne's Revenge* set sail.

It was a painfully sunny day, and I was only up on deck because sitting in my cabin made me want to throw up.

'Look at the horizon if yer seasick, lad,' said Blackbeard.

I leant over the edge trying to feel less green.

A pod of bottlenose dolphins appeared, clicking and squeaking alongside the ship. Dad had done some work with dolphins, because they were supposed to be more intelligent than humans. He'd had high hopes, but they'd resolutely refused to come over to our side.

'Your loss,' I said, sticking my tongue out at them. I gazed out over the unpleasantly glittering ocean, salty spray blowing in my face, and wondered what Dad had meant by *serious consequences*. Whichever way you sliced it, it didn't sound good. Serious. Consequences. I felt even sicker. Well, with any luck we'd rob a ship soon, and I could show Blackbeard I could pirate with the best of them. That'd have to count for something, right?

There was a loud bubbling from underwater. I wiped the sweat out of my eyes and looked down. Green scales shimmered beneath the surface. Were krakens actually a thing? I couldn't remember. The bubbling increased in volume. I gripped the siderail and wished I'd thought to ask.

And then a head popped up. Not the head of a kraken, thank Lucifer. But not a dolphin or a shark either. No. It was the head of a pretty brunette. Then another surfaced from the waves. And another, and another.

'Huh?' I said, because I'm cool like that.

Within an instant all the men were leaning over the edge of the ship, shouting.

'Mermaids!'

''Ello, ladies!'

'Would you care to come visit with us?'

Blackbeard thumped out onto deck and the men rushed back to their posts.

His face lit up. 'Good morrow to you, me darlings,' he said.

'I didn't realise mermaids were actually real,' I whispered.

He raised an eyebrow. 'Yer a demon.'

'Well, yes.'

'Who's travelled back in time. From Hell. And yer surprised mermaids are real?'

I shut up.

Ed went back to chatting up the mermaids.

Late that night, after robbing a vessel full of spices and gold, we set off back to Tortuga. OK, not so much *we* robbed it, as Blackbeard and his crew did. I hadn't passed Cutlass Swordplay 101 yet, so I wasn't allowed to join in the fighting. Not that I was sulking about that or anything.

After weighing anchor, Blackbeard took me off to a crumbling pub called Bessy's Tavern and settled in to tell me stories of the ships that had got away. His filthy, raggle-taggle band of men gleefully spent their ill-gotten gains on rum and were soon staggering about singing very loudly and very out of tune. In comparison, Ed seemed subdued.

'Look at 'em!' he said, waving an arm despondently at the crew. 'Just look at 'em! You ever seen such a dismal sight? So ugly it's hard to believe they ever had mothers.'

'Um.' They weren't exactly a pretty bunch, it was true. Ears had been bitten off, noses had been sliced, and they smelled like last month's laundry.

'That's what I get to see all day and night.' He sighed. 'Pirating ain't all it's cracked up to be.'

'But...sailing the high seas! Being master of your destiny! Pots and pots of treasure! Er...suntans!'

But he just shook his head sadly and ordered another rum.

Three hours and umpteen rums later, Ed was glummer than ever. He continued to moan about a pirate's lot. I was getting a bit sick of hearing about it, to be honest. At least he'd got to join in the afternoon's fighting. Then I had a brainwave.

'Why don't you recruit the mermaids?'

Two bloodshot eyes narrowed at me. 'Yer what?'

'The mermaids. They're really fast in the water. Maybe they could help you with the whole piracy thing. As scouts or something? Plus they'd be nicer to look at than the crew.' I didn't add that roadkill was nicer to look at than the crew.

Ed's eyes lit up. He slapped me on the back. 'Y'know, me boy, yer just might be onta something.'

As it turned out, I was onto something. Something called trouble.

The very next day, the *Queen Anne's Revenge* made a beeline for the mermaids.

And the next thing I knew, Ed had fallen in love with a tubby mermaid called Brunhilda and given up murder and mayhem to set up the Aquatic Creatures' Protection Society.

So much for getting it right. Right and I hadn't even been in neighbouring galaxies. I'd got it so spectacularly un-right my chances of learning how to be a feared pirate had been scuppered before I'd even picked up a cutlass.

And now *consequences* would be coming my way. I hoped they didn't involve krakens.

But when I got home, I didn't even get to leave The Waiting Room.

'Your father's sending you straight on to a new tutor,' said Horslath, a hint of pity in his voice. 'Second time lucky, eh?'

I heaved a sigh of relief. At least I had another chance.

'I hope so,' I muttered. 'Where am I going?'

Horslath consulted his clipboard. 'Transylvania. Cheer up, young man, I hear—'

'It's quite nice this time of year?' I said. 'Yeah, right.' I shook my head. 'But thanks for the thought.'

I gave him a wan smile and hefted my bag back up

on my shoulder.

'Jinx, wait!'

I spun round. My brother Dantalion loped across the room towards me. He looked like a taller, older, better-looking me. If I'd dripped self-confidence. I wished again I could be like him.

'Hey,' I said, 'what are you doing here?'

'I can't come and see my little bro?'

I shrugged.

His dark eyes twinkled wickedly. 'Not even to tell him that a couple of demons by the name of Benny and Arael were suspended from school after being found with strictly illegal white market purchases?'

I perked up. 'You didn't.'

He pointed at his chest and opened his eyes wide. 'Who, me? I had absolutely nothing to do with your friends' new-found love of My Little Pony.'

I burst out laughing. 'Oh, I bet their parents were *furious*.'

'I have a feeling they might've been.'

'Thanks, Dan.'

'No worries. Where you off to this time?'

'Transylvania, apparently.'

'That doesn't sound so bad. Come on, getting private tuition from Dracula? It won't bite.'

'Har har.'

'Seriously, even you can't mess this one up.'

I grinned and shook my head. 'Thanks a lot.'

He gave me a half hug, spun me round back to face Horslath, and gave me a gentle push. 'Go on, get out of here. I want to hear all about it when you get back.'

I strode through the doorway to Earth feeling altogether better about my chances. This time, *this* time, I really would get it right.

4

Vampires Are Bad For Your Health

THE NIGHT WAS black as the inside of a coffin, and just as full of dead people. An unnatural chill seeped up from the castle steps through the soles of my battered trainers, and the howling wind threatened to yank my backpack right out of my hand. Any minute, one of the wavering shadows along the drive would morph into a carriage, ready to whisk me back to the burning home fires, but right then I would've given my right horn to stay where I was.

Yep, back home. I'd only been in Transylvania a week, but things had so not gone according to plan.

The castle door flew open and a tall, skeletal man in a black fur coat, with skin so pale it would've made snow look healthy, stalked towards me.

I edged away.

'Come here, you,' said the Count, beaming at me through his fangs. He threw his arms wide and pulled me into a tearful hug. 'You have made an old vampire

very, very happy.'

I squirmed and blew fur out of my mouth. If only someone else wasn't going to be very, very unhappy with the way things had turned out.

'That's really great, Count. Enjoy your new...you.'

'Oh, I shall, my dear Jinx, I shall. And I have only you to thank.'

That, of course, was the problem.

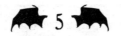

5

Lucifer Gets an Unexpected Phone Call

THERE WAS NO third time lucky. When I got back from Transylvania, Horslath shooed me out of The Waiting Room with nothing more than a sad shake of his green head.

In no time at all, I was back in my least favourite place in the universe: swishing my tail nervously back and forth in the hallway outside Dad's study. *Consequences.* Oh, hellfire. If I'd thought I was in deep water before, this time I was so far below sea level I was swimming with undiscovered species.

I peeked through the keyhole and instantly wished I hadn't. Dad stood in the middle of the room brandishing a golf club, so incandescent with rage there was literally smoke coming out of his ears. Not to mention the flames coming off his wings. I considered hurling myself out of the window, but it's hard to throw yourself to your death when you can fly. The survival instinct kind of kicks in.

Although I sucked so badly at flying I'd probably bounce off a few turrets before hitting the ground, which didn't sound like a fun way to go. I turned reluctantly back to the keyhole.

'Stop shaking!' snapped Dad, lifting the golf club and lining up a putt along the Persian rug. He aimed carefully at the hole, which I now noticed was the open mouth of a bank robber, spreadeagled on the floor like a lion skin. Phew. At least the club wasn't his weapon of choice to beat me to a bloody pulp. Or maybe he was going to multitask. The shot missed by an inch and the robber's head slumped in relief.

Just then, a door carving of a fat goblin poked me in the eye. I yelped. Dad spun round and I clamped a hand over my mouth. Too late. He threw the putter to the floor, straightened his shoulders and bellowed, 'Come in!'

I slipped in, keeping my hand on the doorknob in case I changed my mind about the wisdom of being in the same room as an angry, flaming, eight-foot parent. I was backed up so hard against the wood, gargoyles were nipping at my arms, but that was the least of my worries. I tried to look pitiful, which wasn't hard since I was feeling very sorry for myself at that moment.

Dad threw his hands in the air. 'Two of my very best

men. Heroes of our realm. Giants! And just a few days in your company...' His eyes glittered dangerously. 'How, pray tell, did the infamous Blackbeard come to forgo a life of bloody piracy to become head of the Aquatic Creatures' Protection Society? Mermaids and pirates living together – it's not normal! No, no, never mind. That is as nothing compared to my dear friend Dracula giving up killing innocents and drinking blood, and getting a job working for the Milk Marketing Board! I've seen the poster! All toothy smiles and "Got Milk?" Anyone would think you're working for the other side!'

I gulped. 'Dad, I didn't mean it, the Count just—'

He slammed his fist on the desk so hard a painting fell off the wall. 'Not another word! There are no excuses for your behaviour! None!'

He was right. I felt sick – I'd disappointed him yet again. Why was I so bad at being bad? I didn't bother with puppy eyes this time. I stood mutely, awaiting my fate.

The telephone rang. Saved by the bell! Or, at least, grisly punishment postponed by the bell.

Dad turned, cursing, and snatched up the old-fashioned red dial phone that sat on one end of the desk. 'Yes?' He paused and glared at the receiver as if it had personally offended him. 'Hello? Damn it, who—'

Then it dawned on me that the ringing hadn't stopped. Dad seemed to realise the same thing. He replaced the receiver and we looked in unison across the large mahogany desk.

The white telephone was ringing. For the first time in three hundred years.

MEANWHILE...

God was in His pyjamas, reading the celestial newspaper, *Tidings of Comfort and Joy*, His slippered feet resting on the desk. 'Peace Talks a Success', boasted the headline. God glowed with satisfaction, although this didn't make much difference, since He always glowed anyway. He took a sip of tea and looked sleepily out of the window of His tiny farmhouse, high on a hill overlooking the lush green meadows and sparkling streams of Heaven. Chickens clucked contentedly outside and an old tabby cat stretched luxuriously in a sunbeam on the grass.

He scanned the rest of the paper, then skipped to the sports pages. The Halos were dangerously close to relegation from the Star Hockey Premier League, and He wanted to know if they'd sacked their manager yet. But as He flicked to the back, a tiny paragraph caught His eye, almost lost amongst the endless rejoicing in good news: 'Fistfight On Cloud Nine'.

A fistfight? There was no violence in Heaven. It wouldn't be Heaven if there were. Someone must have made a mistake. But the article explained in detail how an argument over a missing barrel of ambrosia had escalated into a skirmish, ending in bloody noses and bruised wings. Insignificant, by Earthly standards. But unheard of in the celestial realm.

God frowned and picked up the telephone.

Toy Soldiers

GOD AND LUCIFER hadn't always seen eye to eye. In fact, they never had. Dad had been pretty grumpy about being thrown out of Heaven for a while – well, OK, several millennia – but he was fine now. He'd got used to Hell. Our castle was as opulently furnished as any European palace, Pandemonium was a thriving, even pleasant city and the populace bowed down to him at every turn. It wasn't such a bad life. And so, through the ages, they had come to an uneasy truce. Although God didn't like to admit it, my History teacher had once told us, He needed Hell. Where else would He put all the irredeemably bad people?

But they hadn't spoken in years. And now God was on the telephone. Dad picked up with a strange expression on his face, as I huddled forgotten in the corner.

'God?'

A muffled response came from the other end and I wondered absent-mindedly what the voice of God sounded like. A thousand angels singing? Thunderbolts and lightning, very, very, frightening? Morgan Freeman?

'And you,' muttered Dad, sounding sulky. He paused and listened for some time.

'OK,' he said eventually, 'I'll send someone to check it out. That's it? That's the big emergency?'

Another muffled response. A big emergency? I wondered what that could be. World War III? Rise of the robots? Pizza declared a vegetable?

Dad curled his lip. 'Why should I care? Do you lot some good to act a bit more human.' He pronounced the word like it was the worst insult he could think of. And believe me, he knew them all.

Whatever God said wiped the sneer instantly off Dad's face. He swore loudly and at some length, including something about God's mother, which didn't make much sense to me.

'Fine, fine. I'll send my top general to take care of it immediately.' He nodded curtly at the receiver as if God could see him, which, I supposed vaguely, He could, being all-seeing and everything, then hung up and ran a hand through his hair.

I curled my fingers round the doorknob and began to ease the door open before he remembered me. Whatever Heaven's big emergency was, my own personal emergency was far more pressing. The door creaked and Dad spun to face me. So much for that. At least he'd put down the golf club and his wings had stopped flaming.

He flexed his vast black wings menacingly. 'I've had enough of this nonsense. I warned you there would be consequences if you kept failing. Since neither school nor the best tutors in the universe can seem to handle you, I'm sending you to Sharp Point military academy. If they can't make a real demon of you, nobody can. Term starts in three days.'

I gasped.

'Try not to do anything else *Good* before then.' He spat out the word like a bite of raisin cookie he'd thought was choc chip.

My mouth went dry, but I nodded and slunk out of the study.

And walked straight into a snooty reptilian demon waiting outside.

'Ow, my foot!' he said, giving me a look that could've turned buildings to rubble.

I backed away. 'Lord Astaroth! Sorry, you were standing very close to the door...'

The rubble-creating look increased in intensity.

'But, uh, totally my fault, obviously.' I turned and sped off down the corridor before I could get into any more trouble. Astaroth was Dad's second-in-command, a lizard-faced demon who gave me the creeps at the best of times. Great. I was apparently the king of making enemies today.

Back in my room, Loiter took one look at me and tossed aside the Calvin and Hobbes he was reading. 'That bad, huh?'

I nodded shakily.

There was a fluttering of wings and a small bat darted into the room, circled, flew towards me and crashed straight into a pillar. It gave a squeak and slid to the floor.

I bent down and picked it up. 'Bruce, have you been eating Pop Rocks again?'

The vampire bat squeaked pitifully.

'Not very bright, that one,' said Loiter. 'Every time he eats that stuff the noise in his head makes him lose his sense of direction, but he won't stop munching on it.'

'I know. He drinks all my banana milk too.'

Dracula had given me my new pet as a thank-you present. Since following the Count's lead and giving up blood, Bruce had been eating me out of house and turret.

'So what was it this time?' Loiter leant over the edge of the hammock and raised his eyebrows.

I sank to the floor and scratched Bruce absent-mindedly behind the ears. 'I don't want to talk about it. Let's just say it involves mermaids and pirates living together, and mass hysteria.'

'What about Dracula?'

'That one wasn't my fault, I swear. The Count was going to bed one morning when I was having breakfast. He sat down to chat for a minute and asked if he could try my Coco Pops. Was it my fault they tasted so delicious he decided to give up drinking blood?'

Loiter snorted.

'Funny for you,' I said gloomily. 'Now the Count's the

44

face of the Milk Marketing Board and Dad hates me.'

'I'm sure he doesn't,' said Loiter, who was too lazy to ever let anything faze him. Worrying used up too much energy.

'No, he really does. He's sending me to Sharp Point. Children of the demonocracy are never trained to become foot soldiers. It means he's given up on me!' I sniffed back tears.

The sloth's eyes grew wide. 'Sharp Point, really?'

'Really. I'll make a rubbish soldier, I know it. Look at me, I'm already world-class at shooting myself in the foot. I'm not safe around weapons. What am I going to do?'

For once, Loiter seemed at a loss for words. 'Let's sleep on it,' he said eventually. He dropped down to the floor. 'Look, I hate to leave you in the lurch, but I've got an emergency meeting in Texas. Big weapons fair. Those poor arms dealers are always working far too hard. Need to put a stop to it, get them to embrace the delight of sloth.'

I smirked. Loiter really loved throwing a wrench in other demons' plans.

He crouched down beside me. 'But I'll be back in a day or two, probably Fienday morning. We'll think of a plan then, OK?'

'OK, thanks. Wait, morning? You?'

'Well, afternoon at the latest.' He winked at me and

disappeared in a flash of amber light.

I rubbed my eyes. My head hurt and I didn't want to think about Good, or Evil, or anything at all any more. So I did what Loiter would've done, and crawled into bed and fell asleep.

In the middle of the night, something woke me. I peered through the darkness but it was only Bruce. He settled on my head for a moment, squeaking sympathetically, then flew back out of the window. I wished sleepily that I could just fly away. Shame I sucked at flying.

I sat bolt upright in bed and rubbed my eyes. If Dad didn't care what happened to me, why stay? Why *not* fly away? Oh, not literally. But what was the point of any of it if he'd already given up on me? I bet Dantalion wouldn't have meekly trotted off to military school. Suddenly, I knew what to do.

I was going to run away.

 7

Escape From Pandemonium

THE NEXT DAY I made a heroic, daring escape from the castle, rappelling down the battlements and flying across the fiery moat before... OK, OK, so I just walked out the front door and no one batted an eyelid. No one would miss me for three whole days, which was the one tiny silver lining to the thunderous black cloud that was my life. I could be long gone by then. The problem was, long gone where?

I hiked my bag (filled with the Essential Runaway Provisions of banana milk, ketchup sandwiches, Spider-Man comics and a snoring vampire bat) up on my shoulder and stepped onto the arching stone bridge that spanned the moat. Behind me stood Darkangel Palace, the only home I'd ever known, and before me stood freedom. Well, actually, the city of Pandemonium, which was pretty big, was in the way. But *then* stood freedom. Although I wasn't sure exactly what freedom looked like and whether I'd recognise it down a dark alleyway.

I took a deep breath and crossed the bridge into the city. Pandemonium looked like it'd sprung up fully formed overnight, which wasn't surprising, because it had. When the war between Heaven and Hell ended, my dad and all the other fallen angels decided to make the best of things. They were going to live somewhere so beautiful it would make all the other angels jealous. So they magicked up a towering city twice the size of Paris, and ten times as demonically beautiful.

I wandered down Attila the Hun Boulevard, past

spiralling red skyscrapers, the soft white veins in the marble glowing gently in the morning light. Crenellated turrets and golden spires in the shape of scorpions and dragons stretched as far as the eye could see, and a thousand kinds of music leaked out from cafés and bars, weaving a beguiling tapestry of sound with the shouts of street merchants and conversations of passers-by. Way above me in the cloudless pink sky, dozens of flying demons swooped this way and that, pulling rickshaws carrying customers over the labyrinthine streets.

As I gazed up, a gargoyle winked at me from above a shop.'⛤⚇⚇⚉ ⚉⚇⚇⛢⚉⛢⚇⚇, ⚉⚇⚇⚉⛢⚇ ⛧⚇⚝⚎⚇⚇,' it said.

'It *is* a good morning, isn't it?' I replied. A warm flush of excitement began to spread through my belly. I grinned. I wasn't just off to buy textbooks, or meet Loiter for a hot chocolate in a cafe, or on my way to school. I was an outcast, an adventurer, a daring vagabond on life's highway—

Splat.

I was...covered from head to tail in brimstone. I glared up through the red goop dripping down my face. Benny and Arael leant out of a window, cackling.

'Sorry, Stinx, did we catch you? Should watch where you're going!'

'You...My Little Pony lovers!' I growled.

49

It wasn't much of a comeback, but it's hard to be witty when you're soaking wet and smelling of rotten eggs. I stuck up an unimaginative two fingers at them and hurried off to peals of malicious laughter. So much for enjoying the beauty of the city.

I pelted down the boulevard to a café called Devilishly Delicious, snuck into the Gents, and yanked off my jacket and jumper. If I'd been human, the brimstone would've burnt my skin off. As a demon, I was immune to the heat, but not the revolting stench. I tried not to retch as I scrubbed at my face. Some time and several bars of hand soap later, I was still vaguely smelly and my jumper had been consigned to the bin, but it was an improvement. I checked on Bruce, who'd slept through the whole humiliating fiasco.

'Thanks for the support,' I grumbled.

I hitched my bag back up on my shoulder, swung open the bathroom door – and heard a crunch followed by a yelp. *Uh oh.* I pushed the door fully open. A furious-looking Astaroth stood on the other side, rubbing his nose.

'You again!' His lizard eyes narrowed with rage.

I gulped. 'Sorry, sorry!'

Astaroth took a deep breath, like he was counting to ten so he didn't vaporise me, then swept past into the Gents, muttering about brats.

Brilliant. I'd vaguely thought I might spend my first day of freedom wandering through the city, before slipping out of the gates at night, but that suddenly didn't seem like such a good idea. Plan B had been to find somewhere in Pandemonium to hide out – after all, it wasn't a small place. But seeing Benny and Arael and Astaroth reminded me how unlucky I was. Even with a population of five million, I was bound to run into demons I knew from school or the palace, or demons who recognised me because of Dad. I couldn't risk it. There was no way to disappear here.

So...Outer Hell it was. I wasn't quite sure what was out there, since all I knew about it came from Geography books and the little I could see from the palace windows, but I'd have to risk it if I wanted to avoid being caught.

I left the café stoically ready for whatever life outside the gates might throw at me. I was Lucifer's son, after all. I could handle it. Then I nipped back in to get some emergency chocolate cake in case things got really hairy.

Afterwards, clutching a delicious-smelling paper bag, I trotted down the street to the taxi rank.

'Jinx!'

Oh, hellfire, which of my enemies had I run into now? I spun round, trying not to panic. Dantalion sauntered up to me. Phew. A friendly face, at last.

'Hey, little brother, no school today?'

Um. 'Lunch break. Just off to buy some comics.' At eleven o'clock. Gah. I was so bad at lying.

Dantalion, being naturally evil, just raised an eyebrow and said nothing. 'Course you are. Anyway, have fun, maybe see you back home later? For a game of Killer Kannibal Kart?'

'Maybe.' Or maybe not. 'Um, I've got a lot of homework tonight though, so...' I fibbed hurriedly.

'No worries. Don't work too hard! You know how Dad hates that.' He grinned at me and strode off down an alleyway.

Oh yes. I knew how Dad hated that. Right, time to get out of town before I bumped into everyone else I knew in the entire universe. This running away business was harder than it looked. I hailed a rickshaw and, feeling like a spy in some old film, asked him to drop me off at a comic book shop round the corner from the gates, so as not to leave a trail.

We took off and soared up and over Nero Plaza and the Tower of Babel, tiny red shoppers hurrying this way and that far below. The cabbie flapped hurriedly past the Poison Gardens – apparently he was the only person in the city who hadn't heard about my destruction of the Nemesis Tree, which had been known to reach up and pluck rickshaws from the sky before I'd neutralised it – and over the stinking fumes of Brimaeus's Factory, where brimstone was mined by damned humans and converted into everything from medicine to fuel. Eventually we swooped down onto the cobbled alley of Anne Bonny Lane, and scudded to a halt in front of Wicked Comics.

After he'd flown off, I went over my story in my head one last time, then walked as nonchalantly as I could down the road. The air was already cooler here on the outskirts of the city, far from the fiery moat. Outside, it would be freezing. I pulled my black woollen hat and scarf out of my bag and put them on. I hoped they'd serve as disguise as well as protection from the colder climes of Outer Hell.

I'd just turned the corner, nose buried in my scarf, when I saw something not good. In fact, in the list of not good things, it was right up there with razorbug bites, the smell of brimstone and treading on Lego.

The gates were closed.

They towered over me – heavy, black, cast-iron portals reaching a hundred feet into the red swirling sky, mocking me with their unequivocal closedness. *Rats.*

I stood in the street, watching my breath crystallise into little puffs of mist, all the adrenaline leaking out of me like air from a bouncy castle. I'd never been out of the gates before, or even to this side of the city, but I knew they were supposed to be open during the day. After all, hellions – the red-skinned soldiers of Hell that Dad was all ready to turn me into – had to pass through to check up on the kingdom. Maybe security was tighter with God's Big Emergency going on?

Either way, it was horrible timing. I clenched my fists in frustration. So much for being a renegade. I'd have to go back to Plan B, and try to find somewhere in the city to hide out. Unless...unless the gates were just closed *now*. Maybe they were still open at certain times? I decided to go and ask the two hellions standing guard by the door.

The *door*! A barely noticeable, demon-sized exit cut into the right-hand gate. Devil bless you, tiny door. Of *course*, the gates themselves probably hadn't been opened in thousands of years, how could I have been so stupid? The billions of Boneheads – damned humans – on the other side might try to attack the city. Or maybe it'd just ruin the pleasantly warm climate inside the walls.

OK, I could do this, I still had a story. I tried not to think about how rubbish I was at lying, and walked up to the slightly smaller, less intimidating of the two guards.

'Officer,' I said, trying simultaneously to stand as tall as possible and make my voice as low as possible. 'I...'

The guard glowered at me and I stuttered to a halt.

'Where do you think you're going, then?'

Oh brimstone, he'd recognised me.

'Aren't you a bit too *little* to be going off to Outer Hell?'

OK, he hadn't recognised me. I tried not to look relieved.

'I'm a first year at Sharp Point,' I lied, though if he didn't believe me it probably wouldn't end up being a lie at all, which was funny in a twisted way. 'I have to spend a night in Outer Hell, alone. To, er, prove myself.' I looked up hopefully at him, my heart hammering in my chest.

He looked down doubtfully at me. 'Prove yourself, eh? Hmm.' He beckoned the larger guard over. ''Ere, when you was at Sharp Point, did you 'ave to spend a night in Outer 'Ell? Alone?'

The hellion smiled slowly, showing a set of long, sharp teeth. He cupped his hand over the first guard's ear. I strained to listen. 'Nope,' he whispered, 'but it was a prank we used to play on the new boys. Got a good laugh out of it. If they came back alive.' He walked off, smirking.

The smaller guard crossed his arms and tilted his head. Pterodactyls swarmed in my stomach. Was I finally going to have some good luck?

'All right, then, but be careful out there,' he said at last.

55

'Never know what you might run into.' He took a key from his belt, unlocked the door, and waved me through.

I barely noticed the door clang shut behind me before a bone-freezing blast of wind almost lifted me off my feet. I grinned. This was it, this was the real Hell! I'd made it.

I gazed up at the snowy sky. I was an explorer, braving the arctic wastes, armed only with my wits and a pet bat. Someone demons wrote songs about. Someone demons erected statues to. Someone...who realised the door to his doom was still right behind him. I sprinted off into the blizzard before the guard changed his mind.

I decided I'd better do a recce of the area. I was in a place called the Fields of the Damned, that much I knew, a kind of shantytown that hugged the city walls, made up of snow-covered hovels arranged in haphazard alleys that covered the plains of Hell as far as the eye could see. The Boneheads in the Fields weren't dangerous, I remembered – they'd been sent here for minor sins like vanity and coveting their neighbour's convertible. Unfortunately the rest of my knowledge of Outer Hell could've been written on the back of a postage stamp. I wished I'd paid more attention in Geography.

It was impossible to ignore the cold. My teeth were chattering so hard I was worried I might bite my tongue off.

After living in the temperate climate of Pandemonium my whole life, it was a bit of a shock to the system. I stumbled on, the blizzard howling between the shacks and rattling the corrugated iron of the roofs. The ground was frozen solid, but occasionally a burst of blue hellfire flared up through the slush. I ignored it and plodded on.

When I'd gone far enough to feel safe from any guards who might've changed their minds, I stopped and looked back at the city. On this side, the walls of Pandemonium rose up blue and towering, as though they were made of solid ice. I wondered if Dad would notice I was missing before the three days were up. Then I had a horrible thought: Loiter would notice as soon as he came back from Texas. Or at least a few hours later, if he needed to catch up on his sleep, which he usually did. I wondered if he would tell anybody. Stupid. So stupid. I should've told him what I was doing. Or made up some excuse. I'd better put as much distance between me and the palace as I could.

I turned to go, and noticed something I'd missed in all the excitement and flying icicles. Except for the shrieking wind, it was quiet. Eerily quiet. Where were all the Boneheads? It wasn't called the Fields of the Damned for nothing. It was supposed to be swarming with dead humans.

I went over to the nearest shack and peered through

a window, but it was too iced up to see anything. I trod warily down the dirt track of a street, scanning the houses and alleyways, but there was no one to be seen. The silence was starting to unnerve me. I hung a left and then a right. Maybe they were all sheltering from the blizzard. Then I heard a gross coughing noise and spun round. An old man with a long white beard lay in the street, shivering. I backed away and almost walked into a skeletal blonde woman who was pulling her hair and talking to herself. At the sight of me she let out a shriek and ran off. As I trudged on, more and more Boneheads filled the streets. *Of course.* They hadn't dared stray too close to the city. They were scared of demons. Of us. Of *me.*

It was a weird thought. No one had ever been scared of me before. After all, I was about as threatening as a kitten GIF, as I'd proved more than once. My hat kind of covered my horns, but every time a Bonehead came too close, they took one look at my red skin and bolted in the opposite direction. It was a bit unsettling, to say the least.

The Bonehead servants in Pandemonium – like the gluttons who served us dinner, or Dad's bank robber golf partner – looked just like regular humans, admittedly lacking that particular glow that says, 'I'm alive.' The Boneheads out here were no different, but they were much more bedraggled and dirty and frostbitten. Though, looking at the muddy slush and falling-down shacks they lived in, that was hardly surprising.

I racked my brains trying to recall what was on the other side of the Fields of the Damned. Some kind of desert...or was it a fiery lake? Somewhere warmer, at any rate. I didn't want to end up frostbitten too. I decided to head for there.

I was kicking through the snow, lost in thought, when I glanced up and was yanked straight out of my daydream. At the other end of the street stood something I had never seen before – something so unheard of, so impossible, that up until that moment I would've sworn no such thing existed in Hell.

It was a little Bonehead girl.

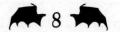 8

A Rare, Lesser-Spotted Dead Girl

CHILDREN ARE NEVER sent to Hell. No exceptions. Fiends aren't allowed to try to corrupt anyone sixteen or younger. And even if a kid does something terrible all by themselves, they get a pass until they're seventeen. Then it's open season. You might not think it, but Hell's governed by a very strict set of rules. Dad's a bit OCD like that.

So what in all the realms was this girl doing here? Had she done something so indescribably wicked they'd made an exception for her? I stared at her. She didn't look indescribably wicked, but then, I suppose, people rarely do. Blonde hair stuck out of her head in two messy plaits, above a snow-stained black duffle coat. Her face was covered in freckles and she looked ten, maybe eleven.

Even weirder, she was skidding along the ice, pretending to skate, and smiling. Like she was *having fun*. Boneheads do not, as a rule, have fun in Hell. After all, that's not what it's here for.

She spun around gracefully, plaits flying, caught my eye, and nearly tripped over. Not wanting to scare her, I started to back away, but she stared right back at me.

A lesser-spotted damned child. Here in Hell. When would I ever get the chance to speak to one again?

My curiosity got the better of me and I took a step closer and tried a smile. 'Hello?'

The girl turned to run, then hesitated. Maybe she was curious too. To someone who'd only ever seen hellions, I realised, I was probably a lesser-spotted demon child.

She stood stock still and silent for a moment, then took a cautious step closer.

'Hey. I'm Tommy, what are you doing out here?' she asked.

I hadn't expected questions. 'I...I don't know,' I said, kicking myself for sounding so lame. I straightened my shoulders. 'I guess I'm exploring. I'm Jinx, by the way.' I held out my hand politely.

'You're a funny kind of demon.' She tilted her head and studied me closely, which was unnerving.

'I am? Well, yes, I guess I am.' I dropped my hand. Even Boneheads could tell what a loser I was. Fantastic. I kicked a stone and tried to think of something clever or interesting to say. My brain refused to cooperate.

The tiny acorn of quiet was threatening to grow into a looming oak of awkward silence when the girl called Tommy walked right up to me. 'You have blue eyes,' she said. 'You look just like the hellions, except they all have red or black eyes.'

'Um, yes. I'm only half demon. Long story.'

She squinted at me and nodded slightly, like she'd come to a decision. 'OK, funny half-demon boy. I like exploring too – you want to see something cool?'

It wasn't like I had anything better to do. 'Sure.'

'Follow me.'

She darted off through the run-down alleyways and past falling-down houses, pausing occasionally to let me catch up. She was fast. I noticed that, unlike me, she had to skip round the thin blue flames that shot up now and then from the ground. I facepalmed mentally – Boneheads weren't immune to hellfire. Obviously.

After a few minutes, we arrived at a vast, ramshackle warehouse, much larger than anything I'd seen so far in The Fields. Tommy slid aside a heavy wooden plank barring the entrance, opened one of the creaking double doors and stepped inside. The room was dark and musty, little streaks of light filtering through the gaps in the roof at least fifty feet above us. Beneath my feet was a packed dirt floor, and the smell of sawdust and grease lingered in the air. I began to feel uncomfortable. What if this was some sort of ambush? Boneheads didn't like us demons much, I was pretty sure of that. I glanced back at the door and was just debating running right back out again when, in the darkness, I heard a switch flip. All at once the room was filled with multicoloured lights and strange tinny music.

I gazed in wonder. It was a fairground. 'What's this doing here?'

'No idea. Guess it must've been someone's worst

63

nightmare. Maybe they fell off a rollercoaster and got their head chopped off. But I like it.'

I smiled, both at the strange indoor funfair and the lack of violent ambush. 'I like it too.'

'This way.'

She wandered off through the stalls, and I followed her until we reached a big pirate ship swing. We climbed up and sat opposite each other in one of the creaky wooden seats. Clouds of dust rose as it jogged back and forth a little with our weight.

'This is so not the way I expected my day to go,' I said, gazing out over the twinkling lights. My stomach chose that moment to rumble loudly and she giggled. I remembered that I hadn't eaten all day and rummaged around in my bag for the ketchup sandwiches.

'Here, are you hungry?' I held one out to her.

'Oh, no thanks. I don't get hungry – or thirsty.' She shrugged. 'Dead thing, I guess.'

I tried not to look too freaked out. Then I realised how unappetising the soggy, bleeding sandwich looked. 'I bet you could eat, if you wanted to.' I pulled out the paper bag. 'How about chocolate cake?'

She took the bag and sniffed. 'You could be right.' She took a mouthful and her brown eyes widened.

'Mmm, that is good.'

I smiled. Corrupting dead people with chocolate cake, all in a day's work. Maybe there was hope for me yet.

Tommy suddenly stopped with the remaining cake halfway to her mouth. 'Wait, how come there's chocolate cake in Hell? Isn't chocolate an Earth thing?' She looked suspiciously at me.

'Oh, it is, but it corrupted so many gluttons that Lucifer decided we should adopt it here too. I'm not supposed to have ketchup, though, so don't tell anyone about that.'

'Right.' She went back to snarfing down the cake. 'Anyway, what are you really doing out here?' she asked. 'Demons don't come to Outer Hell for fun.'

I rubbed my eyebrow, wondering what to say. 'I'll tell you if you tell me why you're called Tommy,' I said through a mouthful of soggy bread. That'd buy me some time to decide what to tell her.

'It's short for Tomasina,' she said easily. 'Tomasina Covelli. Now you.'

Oh. But who was she going to tell, anyway? A hellion? Not likely. 'Well, I...I guess I ran away from home. I thought someone might find me in the city, so I snuck out of the gates. I've never been out here before.'

She looked at me like I'd just grown tentacles. 'Why

would you run away? Whatever's in there has to be better than what's out here. I mean, this *is* Hell,' she said with a chuckle.

I gaped at her. 'How can you laugh? You're stuck in Hell.'

She shrugged. 'What else am I going to do? Like you said, I'm stuck, so there's no point moping around, is there?'

Maybe I was a funny sort of demon, but she was a funny sort of Bonehead, too. I liked her. 'No, I guess there isn't. Do the dodgems work?'

'Yep, come on.'

The silver metallic paint was flaking off the bumper cars and the stripey poles at the back were broken beyond repair on most of them, but Tommy led me straight to one that worked and slid into another. The rubber floor, too, was swollen and torn, but I soon found that only made it better. Who wants a flat floor when you can have little ramps to zoom over?

After the dodgems, we tried out a crooked helter-skelter, a rickety ghost train and finally, the roller coaster. As we screamed our way through the loop-the-loop, arms raised, I tried to remember the last time I'd had so much fun. We staggered out of the car giggling, and Tommy almost fell over before catching herself on the railing.

'You all right?' I said. 'Not going to throw up on me, are you?'

She stuck her chin out. 'Course not. Though...maybe we should sit down for a minute. Don't want you falling over, either.'

'I've got a better idea, let's go sit on that merry-go-round over there.' I pointed to the brightly coloured horses bobbing gently up and down.

'Pfft, that's a little kids' ride.'

'Well, you are a little kid. What are you, ten?'

'Eleven and a half, do you mind? I'm small for my age.'

'OK, why don't we just *relax* on it till we stop feeling dizzy?'

She wrinkled her nose, bunching up all her freckles into a splodge. 'OK, if you really want to.'

We climbed up onto the horses and cantered slowly round the carousel as our spinny heads returned to normal.

I plucked up the courage to ask the question I'd been dying to know the answer to all afternoon. 'So, why are you in Hell? We don't exactly get many kids here. I mean, if you don't want to tell me I understand.'

'The whole thing was a stupid mistake. I really didn't mean...' She sighed and blew the fringe out of her eyes. 'Well, I guess it doesn't matter now. I...'

'Ow!' I started back in shock from where I'd been leaning my hands around the horse's neck. I could've sworn something had just *bitten* me. 'What the...'

'Ouch! Oh – oh *no*.' Tommy vaulted out of her saddle, shaking her hand. Blood dripped from her fingers onto the painted floor.

And then her horse turned and snarled at me, its huge wooden teeth wet and red.

'I think I know why there's a fairground in Hell,' said Tommy. 'Run!'

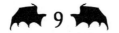 9

The Tale of the Tiny Ninja

INSTINCTIVELY, I FLAPPED my wings, but they were buried beneath my thick winter coat. The only item of clothing I owned that didn't have wing holes, because I'd bought it on Earth. Thanks a bunch, Dracula's tailor. I jumped off the horse just as its teeth snapped at my ankles, vaulted the brass barrier and hared through the funfair, Tommy beside me. But surely those old wooden nags were safely attached to... The sound of thundering hooves finished the thought for me. I threw a glance over my shoulder and gulped as, one by one, the beasts leapt free of the carousel.

We sped back past the pirate ship and under the roller coaster, angry neighing getting closer all the time. Tommy tripped over a tent pole and went flying face first into the dirt and sawdust. I yanked her up by her arm and pushed her on towards the exit ahead of me. It was only twenty feet away now. Almost there. Almost...

Knife-like teeth plunged into my calf and I cried out as the horse dragged me to the ground. I kicked at it

desperately but it wouldn't let go. The others were almost on me too, oh I was so dead – why had I run away, why hadn't I stayed in the city, why was I such a complete and utter *nimrod*?

A thin whistle sliced the air and a star-shaped piece of metal thunked straight into the horse's eye. Half a second later, another took off an ear. It unclamped its jaws from my leg to yowl in pain.

'Come *on*!' yelled Tommy, waving a metal star at me from just outside.

I scrambled to my feet and threw myself out of the door, kicking it shut behind me. Tommy yanked down the thick wooden plank that barred the doors and collapsed in a heap on the slushy ground. There was a thud as something on the other side slammed into it.

I bent over, hands on knees, and tried to get my breath back. The doors rattled and shook, but held.

'Mutant killer carousel horses? Really?' said Tommy, panting.

I shook my head. 'Yeah. Who knew that was a thing?'

A loud crack shook the air and I jumped. The wood was beginning to splinter. Marvellous.

I held my hand out to Tommy who was sprawled on the ground looking like – well, looking like she'd just been in a fight with a herd of carnivorous horses. 'Come on, we'd better get out of here.'

She took my hand and pulled herself up. 'Not even vaguely arguing. Follow me.'

We jogged and slipped through the snowy alleyways until we came to a crooked wooden shack with torn grey curtains peeking out of its only window. Tommy opened the door and I followed her inside.

'Home sweet home!' she said with a quirk of the mouth, waving at the tiny room – and the two lumpy beds, blackened stove and hulking wardrobe that were its only contents. I sank onto one of the beds in relief. At that moment, it was as good as a palace as far as I was concerned.

'What *was* that back there?' I said.

She threw herself onto the other bed face first and propped her chin on her hands. 'No idea, those horses never moved a muscle all the times I've been there. Though I've never climbed onto them before. Guess they didn't like that.'

'No, not them, the flying discs of death – you threw something at that beast chewing on my leg, what was it? Oh, and thank you for, you know, saving me from becoming horse food.'

'Oh – that.' She dug into the pocket of her coat and pulled out a small pointed metal star. 'They're Japanese weapons called hira-shuriken. Back on Earth, I used to be a knife-thrower in a circus. When I...found myself here in Hell, all the things I'd had in my pockets somehow came with me too. I've got six of them.'

I tried to process all this information. 'Not any more,' I said.

'I will have. Every morning when I wake up, all the stuff

in my pockets is exactly the same.' She shrugged. 'Dead thing, I guess.'

'Huh.' We'd never been taught this stuff at school. I guess Boneheads' private lives weren't seen as important.

'Though if I lost my coat, I'm not sure it'd magically appear again. So I make sure I don't.'

'What if you're hurt or something? Do you wake up exactly the same, too?'

'I wish. Why do you think I was running so hard from those horses? We can't die, because we're already dead. But there are worse things than being dead.'

I raised my eyebrows. 'There are?'

'Yeah. One guy got attacked by this thing like a two-headed vulture. Next time I saw him, he was still wandering around – only with one less arm.'

'Yikes.'

'Yeah. And the old woman across the way told me about someone who drowned in a frozen pond out here. The hellions threw him in. Now he's stuck there forever, drowning over and over.'

I shuddered, and for a second I was ashamed of being a demon. But that's what we did, wasn't it? Evil stuff. Boneheads deserved what they got – didn't they? I didn't know what to think so I changed the subject. 'So, you're a real live ninja. Or a real dead ninja, I suppose. Did you really work in a circus?'

'Yeah, I...look, it's a long story. What are you going to do, Runaway Boy? Do you want to stay here tonight?'

'Well, I was planning to go the five-star hotel round the corner...'

She smirked.

'But I stupidly forgot my credit card. Tiny shack it is, then.' I smiled back at her. 'Are you sure you don't mind?'

'Don't be silly. Let me just get a fire started.' She went outside and came back seconds later with an armful of logs which she fed into the stove. After a little while, flames began to lick at the wood and she cupped her hands to blow on it. 'Right, that'll keep us warm enough overnight.' She took off her coat and shoes and climbed into her bed.

I pulled off my backpack and a loud squeak made me start. Bruce! Between the high of the roller coaster and the low of the mutant killer horses, I'd forgotten all about him. I pulled open the bag and he flapped his wings indignantly at me.

Tommy's eyes widened. 'You...have a bat in your bag? Is that some kind of demon thing, like witches and cats?'

I smiled. 'No. But it's also kind of a long story. Don't worry, he's harmless. Why don't you tell me how you went from circus ninja to hell girl, and I'll tell you all about Bruce afterwards?'

'*Bruce?*'

'As in Wayne. You know, bats.'

'Ah. Nice.'

'So, what's your supervillain origin story?'

'Oh, that. Mum was really young when she had me, and my dad disappeared, so I guess she couldn't cope on her own. She tried, for five years, but then one afternoon the circus came to town and she dropped me off with her older brother...' She blinked. 'And never came back. Anyway. Her brother, my uncle Boozy, he was the ringmaster at Fantastic's. He didn't have much choice, so he took me in. Mostly I think he figured a tiny kid riding an elephant would be good for business.' She burrowed deeper under the covers, like the thought of the ringmaster made her even colder.

'But he didn't really like kids. My only friend was Sayonara, the Japanese knife thrower. She's amazing. All swishy black hair and serpent tattoos and fierce eyes. I was only little but I'd seen the way Boozy looked at me. Like he was thinking about leaving me by the roadside at the next stop. So I begged her to teach me. I thought if I was good at something, he'd let me stay. And it worked.'

I stood up.

'Sorry, I'm rambling on.'

'No, not at all. I'm just getting into bed, I'm freezing.' It was true. If my skin hadn't already been red I was pretty sure my nose would've been shining like a beacon. I pulled off my boots and shucked off my coat. 'Really, go on.'

But Tommy was staring at me. 'You have wings.'

I glanced over my shoulder and shook them out like a crumpled black umbrella. 'That is, in fact, true. All demons do. Haven't you seen – ah. Hellions don't have wings, I forgot.'

'But all other demons do? Why don't the soldiers have them?'

'They do, but they're shorn at birth.'

'Ouch. Why?'

'To stop them getting too powerful. Da— Lucifer is clever like that. He likes to keep his subjects under his thumb.' I didn't know why I'd kept quiet about Dad. It was just instinct. Humans were a bit funny about him. Like, terrified-funny. And I really didn't want her to throw me out into the icy darkness. I climbed under the blanket and leant back against the wall. She didn't deserve lies, she *had* saved my life. I promised myself I'd tell her the truth in the morning.

'You were telling me how you became a tiny ninja girl.'

'Yeah. So it was OK for a few years. Me and Sayonara were a good double act, so—'

'Hang on, Sayonara? Doesn't that mean 'goodbye'?'

She chuckled. 'Yeah. It's her stage name. She's really a born-and-bred Londoner called Suze who lives on fish and chips, but don't tell anyone.'

I smirked. 'Her secret's safe with me.'

'Anyway, we worked well together, so Boozy let me stay. But he was still horrible. He made me cook, and muck out the animals' cages, and tons of other stuff, like I was his slave. Once I had bronchitis and told him I was too ill to do the show. He lost his temper and shoved me, and I tripped over a chair and got a huge black eye. I really hated him after that. Then, one day, Zelda, the high-wire act, sprained her wrist. I did a bit of acrobatics and tumbling in the knife show, as well as the throwing, so he made me go on in her place. Problem is, I'm terrified of heights. I saw someone fall off the trapeze and break both legs once, and...'

'Yikes. And he still made you go up there?'

'Yes. And you know, somehow I did it, though I threw up all over Carlo the clown's shoes the minute I got down. But something in me sort of snapped, you know?'

I leant forward. 'And you put a throwing star right

between his eyes.'

She frowned. 'No. No, I was furious, but I never meant to... Oh, I don't know, maybe I did. I was feeding Glinda, the lion we used in the show. She was old and half blind, and usually totally harmless. My uncle came into the cage and yelled at me to clean up the mess I'd made. Like it was my fault I'd been so frightened I'd been sick. And I...I don't know what came over me, but this idea just popped into my head. I did the one thing that drives Glinda crazy, and pulled on her ears. She reared up, ran straight at Boozy...and ate him.'

My mouth opened and closed like a goldfish. 'You fed your nasty uncle to a circus lion?'

She looked sheepish. 'Yeah, kind of.'

I burst out laughing. Dad would've been beyond proud if I'd done something like that. I waved my hand in front of my face. 'Sorry, sorry.'

'I guess it is kind of funny,' she said. 'You should've seen his face when Glinda ran at him. He wasn't expecting *that*.' She shook her head. 'I didn't mean to hurt him, though, I honestly didn't. Even though he almost deserved it.'

'But what about you? How did you end up here? Did Glinda eat you too?'

'No. It was way more embarrassing than that. When I saw what was happening, I ran to the back of the cage and crouched down behind the feed barrel. I was in shock, I couldn't move. When blind old Glinda had finished with Boozy, she padded over and just sat down right on top of me. Squished me flat. She didn't mean to, I know. She just didn't see me.'

'Wow, talk about bad luck.'

'Tell me about it.'

I made a decision. 'Look, there's something you should know.'

'Yeah?'

She looked so relaxed and sleepy I felt bad, but she had a right to know. 'When I said before that we don't get many kids in Hell, well...the thing is, we don't get any human kids in Hell. Nil. Nada. It's a rule.'

'I feel so special. Guess I've always been a rule-breaker.'

'But seriously, the story you just told me...it doesn't make sense. Even if you'd tried really hard to feed your uncle to that lion, you wouldn't be sent here. And the bit about the thought suddenly popping into your mind...that sounds like a fiend to me.'

'A fiend?'

'Temptation demon. They're sent to Earth to corrupt people. But kids are out of bounds.'

She started to unwind her blonde plaits. 'OK, I'm getting confused. There are so many different types of demons. What do fiends look like?'

I pulled a face. 'They're skinny as twigs, and so pale their blue blood shows through their skin. To be honest they kind of creep me out. Oh and they reek. Of brimstone.'

'What does brimstone smell like?'

'Rotten eggs.'

'Ew. Why do they smell of that?'

'They drink it. There's a lot of brimstone in Hell, we mine it here. You know those blue flames you see popping out of the ground? That's brimstone burning – hellfire. Anyway, we use it for medicine and magic and stuff. The fiends drink it in liquid form to enhance their powers of temptation. Which is so gross. You couldn't get me to drink it in a million years.'

'Huh. OK, so there are the hellions who are red-skinned and black-horned like you. And the fiends. Is that it?'

'Oh no, there are tons of different demon aspects. I mean, most of them look like me, but, like, my best friend Loiter, he's a sloth.'

'Wait...a sloth?'

'Yeah. It's 'cos he's been around forever. Most demons look like me, but the demonocracy – the demon aristocracy – they have all different aspects. Dragons and tigers and sloths and lizards. Stuff like that.'

Tommy's eyes grew wide. 'Lizard demons? Great.'

I thought of Astaroth and shuddered. 'Yeah. Anyway, so like I was saying, fiends are the ones who tempt humans on Earth. I wonder if there was a mix-up with you.'

'Curiouser and curiouser.'

'Are you not bothered about why you're the only kid in Hell?'

'I'm sorry, I'm getting sleepy. It *is* weird, but even if there's been some kind of mistake, what am I going to do

81

about it? I can't exactly walk right out of here.'

I thought about Dad. If there had been some kind of administrative error – which was the only answer that sprang to mind – maybe he could help. Then I remembered him playing golf with the bank robber's mouth as the hole. Yeah, maybe not. He wasn't a huge fan of Boneheads.

Still, maybe I could help her. My good deed for the day. Gah, I was such a rubbish demon. But I couldn't help it, I liked her. Plus I was curious.

Tommy yawned. 'Look, I really want to hear your theories on why I won the Hell lottery and about Bruce and everything, but can we do it in the morning? I'm exhausted.'

Her yawn was catching. I pulled the blankets up to my chin and watched the firelight flicker orange along the cracks in the floorboards. Tomorrow I'd see if I could think of a way to help her.

'Course. Night, Tommy. Thanks for the funfair. I had a really good time, you know, until we nearly got eaten.'

A soft chuckle floated through the darkness. 'Yeah, me too. Night, Jinx.'

Blah Blah Secret Plots Blah Blah

BRUCE WAS HANGING upside down from an icicle, swinging back and forth.

'So, what's up with the bat?' asked Tommy.

After a surprisingly nightmare-free sleep, the two of us were building a snowman in the front yard.

'Oh, he's in withdrawal from banana milk.'

'No, I mean, what's a bat doing down here? Is he some kind of demon?'

'Oh yeah, I forgot there are no Earthly animals in Hell. We have our own species, though. Razorbugs, giant killer slugs, the sabre-toothed hummingbird...'

Tommy dropped the snowman's head on the ground. 'The sabre-toothed *what*? Wow, you know how to ruin someone's day.'

'Sorry. Oh, we do have cats, though.'

'Cats? Why?'

I shrugged. 'You try telling a cat what to do. Anyway,

don't worry about Hellish creatures. They won't usually attack a demon, unless another demon commands it. At least that's what I thought, until we went to the funfair.'

She shuddered. 'Yeah, like that two-headed vulture I told you about. I'm in no hurry to see one of those again.'

'Those are called gamrins. But there aren't any in the city.' I picked up the snowman's head, put it on top of the body and tried to pat it back into shape.

'So, what about Bruce?'

'Oh, that.' I explained about the disaster with Dracula and how useless I was at being a demon.

'A vampire eating Coco Pops?' Tommy giggled. 'Is that why you ran away?'

'That was the final straw. Before that I made a giant mess of things at school and with my other tutor as well. My dad was furious.'

'Is your dad a hellion?'

'Um...' I kicked a piece of ice with my foot and thought about the promise I'd made to myself the night before. But if even hummingbirds freaked her out, she'd probably be petrified at the news my dad was Human Enemy Number One. And it was so nice to have a friend for once, even if she was a Bonehead. I decided to keep it under my hat for a bit longer. 'No, he's, um, in administration. In the palace.

Quite high up.' It wasn't really a lie.

'What's it like, inside the gates?' She waved vaguely at the distant city walls.

'Nothing like out here. Not so cold, for starters. The flames from the moat warm the place up. It's...civilised. There are shops and bars and restaurants. Even a golf course.'

'Sounds amazing. Wish I could trade places with you.'

'You wouldn't want to. My dad was sending me off to military school.'

'Wouldn't mind that. I like throwing knives.' She looked wistful for a moment.

'Well, you can't get in and I'm never going back. I'm sick of my dad telling me how useless I am. I'd rather stay out here and freeze to death.' I rammed a stick into the side of the snowman.

'Actually, it's not so bad out here,' she said, gesturing upwards. 'The sky's really pretty today.'

It was true. There was no blue sky or sunshine in Hell, and the days were sometimes not much brighter than the nights. But on some days, the swirling sky shone pink and red and orange, almost like an Earthly sunset. I supposed it made her feel at home.

Tommy's smile vanished. 'Quick! Hellions!' She grabbed

my arm and pulled me into the shack. We ducked down by the dirty window and peeked through the curtains.

A squadron of twelve red-skinned hellions marched down the street towards us, leading sharp-toothed, growling woxes on chains. I swallowed hard. So much for my three-day head start. Dad must've noticed I was gone and sent out a search party.

'What are *those*?' whispered Tommy.

'Woxes,' I said. 'Half wolf, half fox, all deadly.'

Tommy was visibly displeased by this news.

Then I noticed something odd. In the centre of the group strutted a pompous, barrel-chested demon with the head of a bull and fiery orange eyes. The soldiers waved spiked maces at any Boneheads foolish enough still to be in the streets, as the bull-headed demon strolled regally by.

'That's weird,' I said.

'What?'

'The guy in the middle – that's Baal. He's a general and archduke. Demons like him don't usually come to Outer Hell.' And certainly wouldn't be sent out just to find a runaway boy. I heaved a sigh of relief. But my relief quickly turned to curiosity. What *was* Baal doing out here? Maybe it was something to do with God's Big Emergency...

Before Tommy could protest, I opened the front door.

'Come on. I want to see where he's going.'

She shook her head so hard one of her plaits smacked her in the eye.

'Come *on*, we'll stay out of sight, I promise.'

She narrowed her eyes at me. 'Fine. But far, far, out of sight, OK?'

We slunk behind the soldiers at a safe distance as they marched through the snowy streets. After several minutes, they stopped and filed into a stone building framed with pillars. It looked like an old courthouse or town hall.

I hid in a doorway and peered round the corner. 'Do you know if there's another way in there?'

Tommy gave me a death stare. '*In there* doesn't sound like far, far out of sight to me.'

I attempted puppy eyes.

She crossed her arms. '*If* I were stupid enough to want to get in, I'd probably go and check round the back.'

Puppy eyes achieved! Which probably explained why I was such a failure as a demon. I grabbed her hand and dragged her round to the rear of the building. A small rusted balcony teetered precariously to one side. Beneath it stood a pile of old wooden boxes.

'How about up there?'

I clambered onto the crates, grabbed the balcony with my

outstretched fingers and pulled myself up. Then I reached back and hauled up a scowling Tommy behind me. Small flakes of rust fluttered to the ground like metallic dandruff, but the balcony held. At the top was a glassless window, and looking through it I saw a wooden gallery along one side of the room, about twelve feet above the floor. We slid through the window and crouched behind a pillar.

In the middle of the room below, around a table, sat Baal, and another demon with the sleek black head of a panther, who was sipping nonchalantly from a glass of red wine. A third chair lay empty.

'Who's Panther Guy?' whispered Tommy.

'Duke Morax. Some high-up politician.'

Morax tapped his claws on his wine glass. 'How much longer till you get results? Three months and barely a crack.'

I shivered. Morax gave me the creeps. He had a voice like metal scraping on ice.

Baal glared at him. 'We're working on it. My men are doing everything they can. We have a trainload of new equipment leaving tomorrow.'

Working on what? I wondered.

'Anyway, you don't seem to be faring any better with the Nefarium.'

Morax shrugged. 'We're turning the Tower upside down,

but so far nothing. But we'll find it. It's got to be in there somewhere. If you did your job, though, I wouldn't need to bother.' He glanced at the door and lowered his voice. 'Your lack of progress is beginning to anger him.'

I stared at the empty seat. Who were they waiting for? Whoever it was, it sounded like he was in charge. Well, we'd find out soon enough.

Baal growled, his bull's nostrils flaring. 'And you don't think *your* lack of progress is angering him, too? The Wall is a tough nut to crack by conventional means, you know. I've already been through three were-rhinos. If you could find the damn Nefarium, it would make our lives considerably

easier. There has to be something in it about deactivating the Wall.' He took a swig of beer. 'Anyway, we have time. No one knows what's going on, that's the beauty of it.'

Morax's yellow panther eyes glowed strangely. He opened his mouth to speak, rows of sharp teeth glistening, then closed it again, considering his companion.

'Yes, we have time. An eternity, in fact. Oh, eternity, how it drags.' Suddenly he leapt to his feet, batting Baal's glass out of his hand with a roar. 'He is not the only one who grows impatient. I am *tired* of waiting. I am tired of that fool Lucifer, sitting in his palace, running things his way – the wrong way. Our empire is a shadow of its former self. Something must be done!'

I gasped.

'What was that?' said Baal, squinting up into the rafters. 'Pike!'

A soldier ran into the room.

'Send men with woxes to check the rear of the building immediately.'

Tommy and I looked at each other in horror.

Library Cards at Dawn

WE BOTH DIVED instantly for the window, and cracked our heads together. So much for stealth.

'Gah!' Tommy clutched her brow.

I grabbed her arm. 'Come on!'

We slid off the balcony onto the crates with a splintering crash and bolted out of the yard. Swinging left into an alleyway, I heard fierce barking ring out through the cold, still air. I charged on, Tommy at my side, jumping over boxes and skidding along the frozen ground. Not *again*. I was pretty sure life as a runaway wasn't supposed to involve so much, well, *actual running away*.

I dashed round a corner and sucked in my breath. Dead end.

Tommy, a few yards ahead, turned back to face me. 'Quick, back the other—' Her face dropped, slack with fear. She backed away from me.

Uh oh. I spun round. A snarling wox blocked our exit, red fur bristling, saliva dripping from its massive jaws. I scanned the alleyway. Brick walls to my left and right, and a ten-foot chain-link fence at the end. Oh, *hellfire*.

Without a word, Tommy took a run-up, bounced onto her hands and flipped up into the air like an acrobat. She landed on the top of the rattling fence and threw a leg over. 'Hurry, climb up!'

But I was no circus kid. I could barely do a handstand. The wox growled and padded the ground, gearing up to pounce. I yanked my coat off, threw it over its head and ran, flapping my wings as hard as I could. I lifted into the air and flew at the fence, arms outstretched...

And bounced straight off it.

There was a crunch and a whimper as I landed in a painful heap on the ground. I scrambled away, terrified – and then I saw. I'd landed right on the wox and knocked it out cold.

Laughter burst out above me and I looked up to see a guffawing Tommy. OK, so not exactly the most heroic way to win a battle. I slipped my coat back on with as much dignity as I could muster and clambered clumsily up the fence after her.

I narrowed my eyes. 'Not a word.'

We zigged and zagged back through the labyrinthine shantytown until the sound of the woxes' barking faded completely. We still didn't stop for breath until we were safely back inside Tommy's shack, the door slammed shut behind us.

I bent over wheezing, half from the unexpected exercise and half from the unexpected treason.

Tommy wasn't in much better shape – she leant against the wall, her face bright pink. 'Demon dogs bad,' she puffed.

'Tell me about it.' But there were more important things to worry about now. 'Baal and Morax are up to something, we have to find out what!'

She pouted at me. 'I don't think I like being friends with you. That's twice in twenty-four hours we've been chased by monsters trying to eat us.'

'You weren't the one that was almost dog food. But I should've warned you, I don't have the best luck when it comes to...well, anything.'

'Now he tells me.'

'But look, they're obviously plotting against...Lucifer. We have to do something.'

'What wall was he talking about? And the other thing they mentioned, what was it called?'

'The Nefarium. They said it was in the Tower – that's probably the Tower of Babel, so I guess it's a book. A book which apparently deactivates some wall...which makes no sense to me. Well, obviously I know what a wall is, but...' I sat down heavily on one of the beds.

'Why would a book be in the Tower of Babel?'

'Where else would it be except a library?'

'A library? I thought the Tower of Babel was a – actually I don't know what I thought it was, but not a library.' She slid down to sit on the floor.

'Of course, where else would you have books in thousands of different languages?'

'Search me. So where is this library of Babel, somewhere out here?'

'No, it's back in Pandemonium. I don't know what they're up to, but we have to find out more.'

'Do you know who else they were waiting for?'

'Nope.' I scuffed at the floor, annoyed we'd had to run away before we could find out more, especially who the lead traitor was. I tried to remember all the demons I'd seen slipping in and out of my dad's study. 'Maybe Astaroth? He's this creepy, lizardy old demon who's Da— Lucifer's right-hand man. Morax and Baal probably report to him. Maybe he's fed up of being second in command.'

She scratched her nose. 'What about your dad? Why don't you just tell him what we heard? I mean, I know you ran away, but this seems like pretty important information.'

'I can't go back to Dad, he thinks I'm a waste of space. Besides, he'd never believe me. Morax and Baal are two of

94

his closest friends.'

She quirked an eyebrow. 'Some friends.'

I leapt to my feet, suddenly buzzing with excitement. 'We've got find that book before they do! It's clearly the key to whatever they're plotting. Without it, they seem to be stuck. If they find it first...well, it sounds like curtains for Lucifer. But if we can find it and show it to my dad, he'll have to believe me. It's our proof.' I had two days left before I was supposed to start at Sharp Point. Surely if I showed Dad proof of what they were up to, he'd be so pleased he'd forgive me and not send me off to military school. Yes! That's what I had to do. 'We need to go to the Tower of Babel.'

Tommy held her hands up in front of her. 'Whoa, hang on a minute. *We?* Look, I like you and I don't mind if you want to hang around here. But I've seen what happens to people who try to fight back against demons – no offence. I don't want to end up having my toes roasted for the rest of eternity.'

'Oh.'

'Sorry.'

'No, it's OK. Shame, though...' I stretched my arms casually over my head. 'Pandemonium really is a beautiful city. And so lovely and warm. Never mind, guess I'll just have to...'

She narrowed her eyes at me. 'You'd make a terrible poker player. Fine, suppose...'

'Yes?'

'Suppose I did come with you. How would I get into the city? Isn't it only for demons?'

'Demons and serfs. They're our human servants. There are thousands of them. You'd blend in easily. I could say you were my maid.'

She looked like she'd swallowed a razorbug.

'You'd only be pretending,' I said quickly, 'and you said you wanted to see the city. It is pretty cool, actually.'

'Hmm. You *promise* it's warmer? If I get there and find streets of igloos...'

I grinned. 'Promise.'

She rubbed her freckled nose. 'OK, I'll make you a deal. I'll come and investigate this evil plot thing – if you help me find out why I'm here.'

Gah. I'd forgotten all about wanting to help her. But now I really didn't have time to go off on a wild Bonehead chase. I had treason to investigate. Then again, maybe she could help me figure out what was going on. It wasn't like I could tell anyone else, not yet. 'All right, deal. Maybe we'll find answers for that in the library too, come to think of it. That's where they keep the records. But even if I do find out why, I can't promise to get you out of here. No one's ever gone over to the Other Side, as far as I know.'

'The Other Side? Oh, you mean Heaven?'

I nodded.

'All right, but you promise to try, at least?'

'I promise.' Even if it slowed me down, I did still want to help her. And I was curious about why she was here too.

'What about the whole "no kids in Hell" thing? Won't people notice me?'

I shrugged. 'Just keep your face hidden under your hood. Demons never take any notice of serfs, anyway, it's almost like they're invisible. No one will so much as look your way unless you bother them.'

She crossed her arms. 'OK, then, we have a deal. But if I end up as demon toast...'

'I'll be expecting pointy metal right between the eyes.'

'Just so we're clear.'

An hour later, we were standing before the towering city gates.

'Just remember you're a serf,' I said to Tommy. 'Try not to go ninja on anyone.'

'I'll try.'

I puffed out my skinny chest and banged on the door, holding Tommy by the hood of her duffle coat in what I hoped was a suitably masterful manner. To my immense relief, the hellion on guard waved us through without batting an eyelid. I hurried off down the street and in no time we were swallowed up by the crowds. We'd made it.

Tommy pushed me away. 'Oi, let go. Which way...' She trailed off. 'Wow.'

'Not bad, eh?'

Tommy stopped dead, ignoring the crowds of demons pushing by her. 'The buildings look like they've grown straight out of the ground,' she said in a hushed tone. She pressed her hand against the gently glowing red marble of a house. 'How...? There are no joins or bricks. And it looks like it's *alive*, somehow.'

I explained about Pandemonium springing up overnight and her eyes widened. 'So yeah,' I said, 'the buildings pretty much did grow straight out of the ground. At night they glow even brighter, and the streets look like they've been sprinkled with swarms of firebugs. Plus – warmer, right?'

'Yeah,' she said, gazing, rapt, around her. 'Wait – there are no trees or flowers or anything. That's odd.'

'Ugh, flowers. No way. That's Other Side stuff. Lucifer

would never have any of that here. There are some Hellish trees and plants in the Poison Gardens and Outer Hell, but they're all deadly or pointy.' Well, except for the pink flowery Nemesis Tree. I decided to skip that story.

'Hah, of course. It's still amazing. Come on, let's get to the Tower. I'm dying to see what a library in Hell looks like.'

We headed off through the bustling streets, the air getting warmer the nearer we got to the fiery moat and Darkangel Palace. I looked up at its shiny black turrets and wondered if I was being stupid. Maybe I should just go home and tell Dad about Baal and Morax. Maybe he would believe me.

We passed a street corner where a young Bonehead stood, singing an old blues song and playing a guitar.

'His penance is to play guitar?' said Tommy, frowning.

'Yeah, forever. He's quite famous round here. Came out on the wrong side of a deal with Lucifer.'

And he wasn't the only one on Dad's bad side. No, I had to go to the library first and find the Nefarium. Otherwise Dad would think I was just making the whole thing up to get out of going to Sharp Point. With all the trouble I was in, I had to get proof, or he'd never listen to me.

'So that's true?' asked Tommy. 'People really sell their souls to the Devil in return for...I don't know, fame and riches or whatever?'

'Yep. I think Lucifer has fun with that part of the job. He doesn't do it much any more, but he likes tricking humans. He was quite a fan of a play called *Faust*.'

'Huh.'

We hurried on through the city, Tommy still pausing to stare every so often. '⊕⊖⊗⊙⊘ ⊕⊖⊙ ⊙ ⊞⊙⊵⊕⊙⊕⊙⊗,' said a voice.

'Did that gargoyle just *talk*?' said Tommy, pointing at a row of carvings above a deli.

'Yup. They do that.'

'Lovely.' She backed away and walked smack into a tall, red-skinned demon. He instantly raised a hand to slap her. I yanked her out of reach.

'Dantalion!' Of all the lousy luck. 'Stupid serfs, so clumsy. I'll deal with her when we get home.' I fake-scowled.

'Hello, little brother. Having trouble with the help?'

I gulped and glanced at Tommy. Her head was bowed, her hood covering all but her chin. I plastered a grin to my face. 'No, no, everything's fine. Totally fine. Just going to the library for school. *Bo-oring*. Where are you off to? Anywhere exciting?'

He smiled. 'Not really, just going to see some friends. I'm sort of the guest of honour, though, so I've got to dash.'

Of course he was the guest of honour. The only time

I'd get to be guest of honour was at my funeral. I yanked Tommy's arm and backed away. 'OK, then, have a great time! See you soon.'

'Bye.' He turned and strode off into the crowd.

'Sorry,' said Tommy.

'It's all right, just be careful. We don't want any more close calls.'

'Your brother's kind of a big shot, huh?'

'Kind of. He's really cool. He punched a hole through the ozone layer when he was only 119 and then when he was 282, he totally destroyed—'

'Yeah. Great.' She pointed at the deli. 'Any chance we could get some more of that chocolate cake?'

I laughed. 'Sure. Guess we need provisions for our adventure since someone ate all the cake we had. Ahem.'

She looked resolutely unsheepish. 'I'll wait here.'

Five minutes later, I had enough grimberry cupcakes and dreadmeat pasties to last us a week. Hey, a hero can't work on an empty stomach. We left the shops behind and padded down a dark alleyway lit only by the soft glow of the stone.

'What is *that*?' squeaked Tommy, as a scaly, rat-like creature brushed past her ankle.

'Oh, it's only a flaxitt – don't worry, they don't bite.'

'That's OK, then,' she said, not looking remotely OK as

she watched it scuttle up a wall.

I stopped at the end of the alley.

'Now not so much time to stop.' She tried to push me away from anywhere where creepy-crawlies might be lurking.

'We're here.' I stepped out of the alleyway and stuck out my hand with a flourish. 'Nero Plaza. And the Tower of Babel.'

We came out into a large square, surrounded on three

sides by expensive-looking shops and restaurants serving expensive-looking demons. On the far side, wide stone steps led up to a monumental façade studded with three sets of huge ebony doors.

'Whoa,' said Tommy, 'it's like a giant stone wedding cake.'

I'd never thought of it like that, but she was right. The Tower was made up of circular floors, each one smaller than the next, topped off with a pointed rooftop which curled up high into the rusty mists. We climbed the steps and followed a gaggle of demons filing through a smaller entrance cut out of the middle set of doors.

'Remember,' I said, 'act serf-like.'

She nodded.

We stepped over the high threshold into the flickering gaslight of the interior, and tiptoed past rows of tables lined with demons deep in books. Tommy ground to a halt and gaped upwards. The ceiling was hundreds of feet above our heads, with circular mezzanines linked by spiral staircases dotted around the sides of the room. Every inch of wall was covered with leatherbound books.

I dragged Tommy into a long, low room to the side, filled with glass-fronted cupboards marked with the letters of the alphabet. When we got to 'N', I opened the door and began riffling through the card catalogues. After a few minutes I raised a card in triumph.

'Got it! The Nefarium.'

'That seems a bit too easy.'

My shoulders sagged. 'No. Not easy. Not easy at all.' I showed her the card.

'The Nefarium. Byblos. Restricted access only,' she read out. 'What's Byblos?'

'It's where the most valuable and ancient books are held. It's way down in the lower stacks. Those books haven't been catalogued for thousands of years. No wonder they can't find it.'

'How many floors are there underneath?'

'Twenty-four, same as above. The Tower spirals down into the ground like a screw. I think Byblos is on the bottom three floors.'

'Oh.' Tommy scratched her stomach. 'We'll figure something out. Do you—'

There was a rattle and a voice rang out from the far end of the room. A voice that sounded like metal scraping on ice. I held a finger to my lips and squeezed through a gap between the cabinets, pulling Tommy behind me. Footsteps echoed through the room as the voice drew nearer.

We stood very still and listened.

'Nag, nag, nag,' said Morax. 'If it's not Baal, it's the wife.

Can't find the Nefarium, can't find a decent serf these days. Am I supposed to do everything myself around here?'

The demon he was speaking to didn't reply.

'Well, at least we've—'

Bruce chose that moment to squeak loudly. I froze.

'What was that?' said Morax's companion.

For one long, terrible moment, a bone-chilling silence came from the other side of the cabinets.

Then the footsteps echoed out again and my shoulders slumped in relief. 'Probably a booksnake. Don't be so paranoid, Harry. As I was saying, at least we've narrowed it down to the Pagina Prima. Should be able to dig the darned thing up within a week or two.' There was a creak as the door to the library swung open and the voices were cut off.

I realised I'd been holding my breath and took a gulp of air.

Tommy dashed out into the centre of the room and started brushing her clothes frantically with her hands.

I stared at her. 'What *are* you doing?'

'Booksnakes? Really? Are there any animals in Hell that aren't going to try to eat me?'

'Don't be silly, booksnakes are harmless. They only eat books.'

She stopped flapping. 'Hmph. Anyway, that was pretty

nice timing. Maybe you're not as unlucky as you thought. Do you know where this Pagina Prima is?'

'Yes, but it doesn't help much. It's the furthest reaches of Byblos, the bottom floor, so we've narrowed it down a bit. The thing is, it's like a labyrinth down there. Be easy to get lost.'

'Hmm. Do you know the story of the Minotaur?'

'Know it? He was a cousin of mine.'

Her eyes widened. 'Wait, what? I thought that was a myth?'

'Bet you thought Hell was a myth too, before you came here.'

She tilted her head to one side. 'Huh. Yeah, I suppose I did.'

'Humans get their legends and myths all mixed up. History is kind of like a game of Pictionary, except the drawings are all really bad so everyone guesses wrong. You'd be surprised what's true.'

'Wow. You'll have to tell me more about that when we get out of here. I haven't seen a pitchfork yet, so I guess that myth's false. Anyway, in the story I know, Theseus leaves a trail of thread so he can find his way out of the labyrinth. We could leave some clues for ourselves so we don't get lost.'

'Good plan, Batman.' I squinted at her. 'You're very

adventurous all of a sudden, for someone who's scared of booksnakes.'

She pulled two hira-shuriken from her coat and struck a pose. 'Hey, I like a good adventure as much as the next tiny ninja girl.'

I grinned.

'And, well, I hadn't met a single kid in Hell till you turned up. Now I know why. So even if you are all angsty and demonic, it's quite nice to have some company.'

'I am not...*angsty*.'

She clutched her chest and raised her eyes to the ceiling. 'Poor me, I'm such a failure as a demon. If only I could be an evil supervillain so my dad would be proud of me.'

I snorted, despite myself.

'So, Captain Doom, what's next?'

'Next, I look into the mystery of you. Then we'll set forth on our quest for buried treasure.' I hefted my bag up on my shoulder. 'It's going to be a long, perilous journey. I'm glad we brought snacks.'

MEANWHILE...

'She does it on purpose!' stormed Lucifer, staring at the letter clenched in his fist. '"Having an absolute ball. Greek men are so charming. Such a shame you're not here. All my love, Persephone. Kiss kiss." Why does she torment me so?'

Loiter looked out over the golf course. 'Because she knows you enjoy it.'

Lucifer sighed. 'I can't help it. She's sweet and funny and smart...and manipulative and scheming and vengeful. She's my perfect woman!' He stuffed the offending letter in his pocket, picked up his club and swung it angrily at the green. The golf ball flew through the air and plopped straight into a bunker. Lucifer growled. His caddy, a mountainous Bonehead who'd been Al Capone's second-in-command, took a nervous step backwards.

'Texas was good, by the way,' said Loiter, a mischievous glint in his eye.

'You did not just tell me that. I'll never hear the end of it from Gaap. Arms dealers are perfect prey for the Patron Demon of Greed, then you swan in and make them too lazy to care about spreading destruction all over the globe.'

Loiter chipped languidly. His ball sailed through the air and landed neatly a foot from the flag.

'And whilst we're at it, if you had more sense you'd let me win,' said Lucifer.

108

Loiter ignored him. 'How are things going in the Mariana Trench?'

Lucifer perked up. 'I have high hopes. Some really terrifying sea monsters coming along down there. Few years and they should be able to cause a nice bit of havoc.'

'Could be trained to eat a few charming Greek men, I bet.'

Lucifer grinned. 'That's the best idea I've heard all day.'

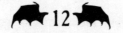

The Game Show of Doom

I LEFT TOMMY in a dark corner of the main library, reading *The Garden of Eden: A Snake's Story*, saying it was best if she kept hidden. Which wasn't untrue, but I also wanted to use Dad's influence to get the librarian to let me search the records.

I pushed through a small door bearing a brass plaque saying 'Damned Archive' and went up to the desk where a librarian with deep purple skin was hunched over a book.

'Excuse me. I need to look up information on one of our house serfs.'

She gave no sign that she'd heard me.

'In Darkangel Palace.'

Her face shot up out of her book.

I smiled at her. 'I'm looking for a Tomasina Covelli. With a C.'

It wasn't unusual for demons to look up serfs' records. That way, we could make sure the punishment fit the crime. Slothful Boneheads were given back-breaking labour mending roofs and gutters from morning to night.

Gluttons were put to work serving dizzying arrays of delicious food they would never get the chance to taste.

'Of course, sir, follow me.'

She led me behind the desk and into a room not unlike the one I'd just been in with Tommy, cabinets stretching far into the distance. Only this one was so long I couldn't see where it ended. It took us ten minutes just to walk to the Cs. I thanked my lucky stars Tommy's surname didn't begin with Z.

'Call if you need anything!' said the librarian with an insincere smile, disappearing back off to her book.

I pulled out a drawer marked 'Cov', sat on the dusty floorboards, and began to search. After half an hour of paper cuts and sneezing, I'd been through every single card marked Covelli, and none of them were a Tomasina. Curiouser and curiouser, as Tommy would've said. But then again, maybe not. After all, if she was in Hell by accident, it'd make sense there were no records of her. Then I had an idea.

I slotted the drawer back into its shelf and went back to the front desk.

'Find what you were looking for?' asked the librarian.

I put on a haughty voice. 'No, I didn't. Absolute disgrace! Imagine losing records like that. I'll have to tell

111

my father about this.'

She shot up out of her chair, knocking her book to the floor. 'Oh, please don't do that! Are you quite sure it wasn't there?'

'Absolutely.' I softened my tone. 'Well, I'd hate for you to get into trouble. Tell me, do records often go missing?'

She hesitated, not sure what the right answer was.

I smiled at her. 'It'll be our secret, I promise.'

'Well...yes. To be honest, it does happen from time to time. Billions of names to keep track of, and sometimes the booksnakes get in there....'

I ratcheted my smile up a few more notches. 'What about mistakes? Do Boneheads ever get sent here by accident? You know, instead of the Other Place?'

Her face relaxed. This, I knew, wasn't her job. She couldn't get in trouble over administrative errors. 'It's been known,' she said darkly. 'Not often, you understand, and those idiots in Admin always try to hush it up...but yes, it's happened a few times.'

That's what I needed to know. 'Thanks for your help.' I noticed a box of chalk on the counter. 'Mind if I borrow one of these?'

'Um, no, help yourself.'

I took a piece and turned to go.

'You won't mention the records to your father, will you?' she called after me.

As if he'd care. 'Don't worry, your secret's safe with me.' I was halfway out the door when I realised I'd forgotten the most important thing. This cloak and dagger stuff is harder than it looks, I'm telling you. I spun round. 'Almost forgot, Dad also needs me to pick up a book for him from Byblos.'

'Oh, of course.' She rattled through a bunch of keys hanging behind her on the wall and passed me what looked like a locker key, brass with a cylindrical end.

'Thank you.'

I pocketed it and strode off back to the main library to give Tommy the news, or lack of it. But when I got there, she wasn't where I'd left her. Oh, hellfire. I scanned all around me, trying not to panic. Demons of all shapes and colours thronged the library – but there were no annoyingly perky Bonehead children to be seen. Had someone discovered her? Had she been hauled off to— *Ow!* A book landed on my head and fell onto the floor in front of me. *How to Summon a Demon in 12 Easy Steps.* I looked up. Tommy giggled down at me from halfway up a ladder.

I gritted my teeth. 'I thought you were scared of heights.'

'Pfft, trapeze heights, not a few feet up.' She pushed the ladder and it trundled along the stacks. 'Look, it rolls!' She gave me a delighted grin.

Tommy seemed to be able to have fun anywhere. 'You are so childish.' I rubbed my head grumpily.

'Of course I am, I'm a child,' she said, sticking her tongue out at me. She climbed back down to floor level and hopped off. 'So, did you solve the mystery of me?'

'Not exactly. But I did find out that people sometimes get sent to Hell by accident. So I'm guessing they just made a mistake, and you're not superevil or anything. Hope you're not too disappointed.'

'Ha ha. Was I in the record books?'

'Nope. No Tomasina Covelli listed at all.'

Her face lit up.

I raised an eyebrow. 'And this makes you happy because...?'

'Maybe I like being all mysterious.' She smiled. 'And, you know, at least it didn't say *Tomasina Covelli is doomed to Hell for all eternity for feeding her nasty uncle to a lion. End of story. No mistake.*'

'Good point.'

'Anyway, let's get going. We don't want Scary Panther Guy to get his hands on that book before us.'

'Right. Yes. Follow me.'

We picked our way round the edge of the room, past the

114

tables of studious demons and out of an exit right at the back which led to a small wood-panelled lobby with a pair of double doors leading off it.

Tommy took a deep breath. 'Twenty-four flights down,' she said. 'This is going to be fun.'

'Well, if you fancy a bit of exercise.' I pressed a brass button to the side of the doors. 'Or we can just take the lift.'

She stared at me. 'The lift?'

'We're not complete savages, you know.'

'But everything here's so old-fashioned.'

'We aren't always up to date on everything from Earth, true. But lifts were invented hundreds of years ago.'

There was a low ding and the doors slid open, revealing more wood-panelling and a low velvet bench seat.

I waved my hand. 'Humans first.'

A slightly stunned Tommy got into the lift and I followed.

'Depths of Hell, coming up.' I took the key the librarian had given me from my pocket and twisted it into the round keyhole under the lowest button. The doors whooshed shut.

'We need a key to get down there?' She quirked an eyebrow. 'Which you just happen to have?'

'Byblos is a restricted area – you need a key to get to the bottom floors. Charmed the record-keeper into giving it to me.'

She smirked. 'You *charmed* her? Right.'

'Shut up.'

There was a slight judder and we began, creakily, to descend.

Tommy sat down and folded her arms. 'So. How are we supposed to find something that dozens of minions haven't been able to dig up?'

My eyes widened. 'Don't say that word!'

'What word? Minion?'

'Stop it! Yes, that word. It's really rude. Demons might be Lucifer's subjects but they aren't his slaves. Or at least, they don't like to think so.'

She grinned. 'Now I know how to insult a demon. The things you learn. Are there any other Evil Rules of Etiquette I should know?'

I thought for a moment. 'Don't ever say Persephone's name in front of anyone, unless she permits you to. That's Lucifer's wife. Centuries ago she was called She Who Must Not Be Named and anyone who said her name was put to death.'

'Whoa, she sounds like a badass.'

I smiled. 'She is. I think even Lucifer's a bit scared of her. Oh and it's against the law to kill a gargoyle. Gargoyles don't do anything apart from hop around cracking jokes and singing. I think Lucifer has a soft spot for them.'

Tommy nodded mock-seriously. 'I shall attempt not to accidentally murder any amusing stone statues. So...how are we supposed to find an ancient, special book that even Morax's *gang* haven't been able to turn up?'

The lift squeaked ominously and I sat down beside her. She had a point. How *would* we find the Nefarium?

'Well, we can discount anywhere Morax and co. have already searched. They sound like they've been at it a while, so that'll narrow it down. Apart from that, I'm not really sure. But I have a feeling an artefact as important as this book seems to be isn't just going to be sitting on a shelf somewhere.'

'Yay, hidden bookcases! Secret tunnels! Sneaky trapdoors!'

I couldn't help smiling. 'Could be. Something like that, anyway, I reckon. So it's not like we have to search every shelf. We just need to look for anything out of the ordinary.'

She raised an eyebrow. 'Something out of the ordinary...in the darkest depths of the Tower of Babel which is actually a library. With booksnakes. And demons. In Hell. Okey-dokey.'

'You know what I mean.'

The lift squealed and shook and I was just wondering

whether taking the stairs might not have been a terrible idea after all, when it shuddered to a halt. I stood up, pulled Tommy to one side and peered out as the doors opened.

'Phew.' There was no one there. The lift led out onto a small landing with a door leading off it marked *Byblos Two*.

'Come on.' To the right of the door was a stone staircase. We trotted down past another landing with a door unsurprisingly marked *Byblos One* and came to the bottom floor. The Prima Pagina. I looked at Tommy and held a finger to my lips. She nodded.

We crept out and found ourselves in a...cave?

'Well, this isn't creepy at all,' said Tommy.

There was no lobby – the door led straight to the stacks. But this was like no other part of the library I'd ever visited. We gazed up at the ceiling, or rather, the roof, of a vast, echoing, dark cavern. Lamps hung from stalactites, and mahogany bookcases stretched off into the distance, curving this way and that around stalagmites branching up from the floor. Piles of broken books lay sadly on the floor, as though they'd been pulled hurriedly from shelves. Silvery spikemoths and deep blue inkbats fluttered around the glow from the lights.

'Who knew the Prima Pagina was also the Batcave?' I said.

She gave me an evil glare. 'More harmless Hell beasties?'

118

'Ah. The inkbats, yes, totally harmless. Although they might spray you with ink if they get scared. The spikemoths can sting, so, er, probably best to keep away from them. They're not fatal or anything, though,' I added quickly, as the evil glare approached supervillain proportions. 'Kind of like a bee sting. And if looks could kill, you'd have annihilated them by now. Come on, judging by all those books that've been yanked off the shelves, they've searched this area already.'

We set off through the winding stacks, Tommy glancing nervously above her head every two minutes, me keeping my eyes peeled for any sign of Morax and his men. The air smelled of old books, like vanilla and violets, but underneath was another scent, one I couldn't quite make out. I hoped it wasn't Morax's aftershave. Each time we rounded a corner we came across more empty shelves and torn books. Astaroth – or whoever Morax was working with – was definitely in a hurry to find this Nefarium, whatever it was.

'The more I think about it, the more it makes sense for Astaroth to be the ringleader,' I said.

'Yeah?'

'As Lucifer's second-in-command, he knows the realm as well as anyone. And he's in on all the politicky stuff. I bet

119

he'd know who to pick to plot against Lucifer.' Plus he gave me the creeps, with his reptilian sneer and scaly greyish wings. I could totally imagine him betraying Dad.

After half an hour, we reached the other side of the main cavern and came to a stop in front of six arched wooden doors, numbered in brass Roman numerals from left to right.

Tommy rolled her eyes. 'Great. It's like an evil game show. Behind Door Number One, demons. Behind Door Number Two, booksnakes and spikemoths. Will our heroes

correctly choose Door Number Three before they get eaten by monsters? Tune in to find out!'

I chuckled. 'Let's start with Six. With any luck they started with One.'

'OK, but if I get eaten...'

'Yeah, yeah.' Like there was really any danger in a library.

I pushed the door open and walked into— 'Aaaarghh!'

'Jinx!'

My feet paddled in thin air and I hung onto the door handle with all my might. Because behind Door Number Six, there was nothing at all – the floor simply dropped away. So far away that I couldn't see the bottom. I screamed again.

'Jinx, give me your hand!' Tommy hung onto the doorframe and reached out towards me.

I swung my free arm up and grabbed her fingertips. I didn't dare pull too hard or I'd yank us both into the abyss. Gently, gently. The door creaked ominously, and then swung slowly – horribly slowly – back towards her. Just a little nearer...a few more inches... I threw myself out onto the floor of the cavern, landing on my knees with a crunch.

Tommy put her hand on my shoulder. 'You OK?'

I nodded, not daring to speak. I was pretty sure it'd come out as a squeak.

She frowned at me, scrunching up her freckles. 'I don't understand, why didn't you fly to safety?'

I stood up and crossed my arms, my cheeks hot. 'I suck at flying, all right? I'm a rubbish demon in every department. I can fly a few feet, but whenever I try to go any higher I bash into walls or go into a tailspin. You saw what happened with the wox in the alleyway. I panicked and didn't trust myself to fly out of there.'

'Oh. Sorry.'

Now I was embarrassed at being sulky, as well as useless. I could still feel the stomach-dropping sensation of my legs pedalling in thin air. I took a deep breath and tried to smile. 'No, I'm sorry, it wasn't your fault. So, behind Door Number Six, instant death. Excellent. Moving on.'

Tommy wrapped her hand round the handle of Door Number Five as gently as if it were an egg. Nothing happened. She pushed it open an inch and peered through the crack. 'Well, there's a floor.'

'Always a bonus.'

She pushed it all the way open. 'And shelves. This one, Captain Doom?'

I peered inside. A long, rocky corridor, lined on either side with bookcases, snaked off into the distance. The air was warmer here, and smelled musty. It was narrow, but the ceiling was still at least twenty feet high, with the same glass lamps hanging from outcrops here and there. It seemed safe enough, but I was much warier about libraries than I'd been five minutes ago. Still, we had to start somewhere.

'OK.' I elbowed her in the side. 'And stop calling me Captain Doom.'

We headed off into the gloom, pausing to test any sticky-out pieces of rock or odd wooden lumps on the bookshelves that looked like they might lead to secret passages. After a few minutes, we came to a fork.

'We should split up,' I said.

Tommy's eyes blazed fire. 'We should what?'

'Joke, joke, stop hitting me.'

I took the piece of chalk from my pocket and wrote a large 'X' on the bookcase, then headed down the left fork. Soon there were more forks, and more. I studiously marked an X for each turn we took.

'Have to say, starting to get a bit claustrophobic,' she said. 'We must be a really long way from the cavern by now.'

She wasn't wrong. And we still hadn't found any cunningly hidden secret passages. 'Break for cake?'

'I thought you'd never ask.' She slumped to the floor and leant against a bookshelf. And screamed. A tiny ink-stained booksnake writhed on her head. I grabbed it and tossed it away.

'Sorry. But, harmless, really.'

She stuck her hand out. 'Cake. Now.'

I dug into my backpack and handed her the chocolate cake before she started hitting me again.

'Are you sure you're right about this secret passage business?' she asked, mouth smeared with crumbs.

'No. Not at all.'

'OK. Just checking.'

Bruce's little head popped out of my bag and he yawned. He hopped onto my shoulder.

'Hello, trouble.' I chucked him under the chin and he flew off to explore. 'Don't get lost!' I called after him. He swooped up to the ceiling to make friends with the inkbats.

'Thank you,' I said to Tommy, 'for coming with me. You really didn't have to.'

'And miss all the delights of the city?' she said, waving at the dingy corridor. 'Never. Besides, you kept your promise to try to find out why I'm here. Maybe we'll still find out more.' She stood up and brushed the crumbs from her face. 'That's better. Onwards and upwards!'

We trudged off down the stacks, Bruce following several feet above our heads. I began to wonder whether we'd have to spend the night here. We'd come a long way and were still no closer to finding the Nefarium. Maybe it was

124

behind Door Number Four. And what was worse, I really needed to pee. Dead girls didn't seem to have that problem.

'You go on ahead,' I said, embarrassed, 'I just need to, um...'

'No way, I am not...oh. Right.' She marched off a few paces, took another fork, and I heard her footsteps come to a halt on the other side of the shelves. She started humming.

Nope, not awkward at all. I slipped behind the shelves with a sigh of relief. If this were a film, I thought, I'd totally find the secret trapdoor now. But no such luck.

A minute later, much more relaxed, I hurried off to find her. But she wasn't there. Not this again. I searched the stacks for rolling ladders and found one, but she wasn't on it. That wasn't good.

'Hey, come back!' A blonde head popped round the corner.

Thank the Devil. 'Stop disappearing!' I said, annoyed.

'It's Bruce, he's gone!' She pointed at the ceiling.

Several dusky blue inkbats were fluttering about, but there was no sign of a black vampire bat.

To make matters worse, I heard voices in the distance. 'Oh, no.'

Tommy's brown eyes grew wide. Before I could stop her, she'd shot up the ladder and slid into the gloom on the top of the bookcase. I scurried up after her and was almost at the top when two hellions appeared beneath me. I froze, one foot in mid-air. They hadn't seen me. Yet.

Keep on walking, I thought. Please.

'Bloomin' book ain't anywhere,' said one of them as they passed.

'Must be in the sixth room, then,' said the other.

They carried on and disappeared round the bend. I let out a sigh of relief.

Tommy gave me a quizzical look. I shrugged. There was no sixth room – just a bottomless chasm. So if it wasn't here, where in Hell was it? I clambered up onto the top of the bookshelf and leant back against the wall.

'So they have searched this room,' she whispered. 'And all the others, by the sound of it. Now what?'

'I don't know. Either it's not here at all, or they've missed it. But I really don't fancy getting lost in these caverns.' I thumped the bookcase with my fist. 'I'm going to have to go home and ask my friend Loiter for help. I didn't want to have to do that. Ah, well. Come on, let's find Bruce and get out of here.'

The problem was, it wouldn't be easy getting Tommy into the palace without being seen. Rats.

'Bats!' said Tommy.

'Huh?' I peered up but there was still no sign of Bruce. 'What?'

'Those bats, inkbat things, they went through a hole in the cavern wall. Look, up there!'

I peered up and saw three of them flit through a gap in the rock. Tommy crawled along the dusty bookshelf top and I followed, until we found ourselves below a jagged oval hole in the rock. Light filtered through from the other side.

'Door Number Five?' she said. 'Or secret room of treasure?'

'Knowing my luck, another bottomless abyss.' I stood up and peered through the gap. But the room on the other side was not a library, or a pit of doom. It was some kind of indoor courtyard with a broken fountain.

'That's weird.'

She nudged me aside. 'Secret room?'

'Don't think so. There are no books in it.' I cupped my hands round my mouth and called out for Bruce. There was a squeak and he appeared from behind the fountain.

'There he is. Bad vampire bat!' She waved her finger at him.

I smiled. 'Want to check it out anyway?'

'Sure. Fortune favours the stupid. Or something.'

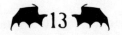 13

We Get in Deep Water

I SQUEEZED THROUGH the narrow slit in the crumbling wall, getting covered in rock dust in the process, and dropped down onto the other side. It was a round room, no larger than my bedroom, with a broken mosaic floor and two doorways leading off it. The strange scent I had noticed earlier was stronger here. I sniffed the air. It smelled a bit like sea water. Weird.

Bruce flew over and settled on my shoulder.

'You are either the key to the treasure,' I said, 'or the one we're going to blame when we come to a sticky end.'

He opened his eyes wide and tried to look innocent.

'At least we don't have to choose doors again,' said Tommy, dropping down next to me. 'That one's blocked by a rock fall.'

'OK, but hang on, you sure there's nothing here?'

She went over to the dried-up fountain and felt around inside. 'No hidden levers there. Just a few dregs of water in the bottom.' She flicked her wet hand at me.

'Ow! Stop it!'

'Don't be such a baby.'

I rubbed my face grumpily. 'That stung. You must've flicked a bit of rock at me. Anyway, onwards and...whereverwards.'

She jogged off through the open doorway.

'Wait for me!' I coaxed Bruce into my backpack, tied it shut, then hurried after her down a low corridor carved out of the rock. The air began to get clingy and damp, and the odd smell stronger. I shivered. Something wasn't right about this place. I hoped there were no more abysses in my near future. At the end of the passageway, I stepped cautiously out and found myself on a rocky overhang above a high, narrow cave.

A high, narrow cave that was occupied by a gaggle of hellions and a certain panther-headed duke.

I grabbed Tommy's sleeve and we crouched down out of sight and peered over the edge. Was this the place we'd been looking for? Or were they as lost as us?

Morax seemed to be arguing with the captain of the hellions.

'Give us a little time, sir, and we can build a bridge of some sort,' the captain said, his red face stern, 'or get a pump to suck out the water.'

Huh?

Morax waved a black paw to his left. And then I saw it. The cavern was actually much bigger than it appeared – but half of it was taken up by a deep, wide overhang, only a couple of yards above the ground. And beneath it was a pond. A gap of about two foot – too narrow to fly through – divided the roof of the overhang and the stagnant brown water.

'We don't have time,' said Morax. 'Would you like to be the one to tell our illustrious leader that we found the Nefarium and somehow took several days to get it to him? Because your men were too cowardly?'

The captain sucked his cheeks in like someone had insulted his mother. 'My men are the bravest lads in the army, sir. Dragon Division are famous for their fearlessness.'

'So prove it to me. Get me that book.'

'Ugh,' whispered Tommy. 'So we found the secret room, but they got here first. That is seriously annoying.'

It was. 'It must be in the water. Weird.' I tilted my head, but we were too high up to see all the way under the overhang.

The captain's shoulders slumped. 'Yes, sir.' He turned to the soldiers. 'May I have a volunteer?'

Three demons immediately took a step forward.

'Thank you. Carthus, you are tasked with delivering that

book,' he pointed beneath the overhang, 'safely back to us. Under no circumstances must it get wet.'

Carthus nodded his horned head. 'Yes, Captain. It would be my honour.'

'What's all the fuss about?' whispered Tommy.

'No idea.' If the water was very deep, it'd be tricky to swim across without getting the book wet. But not impossible. I shrugged. 'Killer mermaids?'

The soldier called Carthus, who was dressed in the usual light grey leather armour, walked up to the edge of the water and plunged straight into it. He was built like a were-rhino, and the water only came up to his thigh. So it wasn't deep at all. Then what was the big deal?

'Oh, no.' My hand flew to my mouth.

The big deal was that he began to smoke – immediately.

He let out a low hiss – then strode on ahead, head bent below the overhang. The smoke curled off him, rising up from the water like grey serpents.

'What's going on?' said Tommy.

I felt sick to my stomach. 'That isn't just water. It's holy water.' That's what the strange smell had been.

'So?'

'It's toxic to demons, like brimstone and hellfire are to humans. There must've been holy water in that fountain, too. That's why it stung me.'

She smirked. 'Guess that means I have one over on you demons.'

But then the tank-like Carthus began to whimper, and Tommy's smile vanished. His step faltered, and he glanced back over his shoulder towards dry land. I sucked in a breath. His face twisted into a mask of panic and horror. He tried to turn back, but his legs buckled and he let out a shriek that made me want to throw up. And then he fell, and the pool of holy water turned red like he'd been swallowed by a school of bloodthirsty piranhas.

Tommy put her hand to her mouth and retched.

'Hmm,' said Morax, cricking his neck. 'Looks like you were right, Captain. We're going to have to pump the water out. I'm going back upstairs. Find me when it's done.' He spun round and left through an entrance in the rock without a backwards glance.

The captain ran his hands through his hair and grimaced at his men. The pond bubbled unpleasantly one last time, then fell still. 'You heard him, lads, let's get going. There's a pump back at the barracks.' They all trooped out of the cave.

Tommy sat back against the rock. 'Well, that was gross.'

'Yes. Yes, it was.'

And that was the kind of thing Dad was sending me off to do, I thought, by dispatching me to Sharp Point. He really didn't care about me at all. I leant back and hugged my knees.

'You all right?' said Tommy.

'Yeah. Yeah, I'm fine. OK, look, they've gone, but we have you, ninja secret weapon. Humans are immune to holy water! So, let's go get that book.' I forced a smile onto my face.

'It better not be acid,' she said, lifting herself over the edge of the overhang and starting to climb down.

At the bottom, I told her to wait whilst I checked the exit. I found a long corridor that led into, I presumed, the library behind one of the first four doors. But the hellions had all gone. I crept quietly back to the cave and found Tommy sticking her toe in the water. There was no smoke.

'All good?'

She looked like she was about to jump out of a plane – half excited, and half like she might throw up. 'Yeah.'

From down here, we could see all the way under the overhang. On the far side of the pond, perhaps forty feet away, stood a stone pedestal – and on it sat a large book. The Nefarium.

Tommy took a step into the pond. She was much smaller

than the soldier, so the water came up immediately to her armpits. But there was no screaming. I breathed a huge sigh of relief. She splashed on hurriedly then pulled herself up onto the raised pedestal.

'OK?'

'Yep! No problem.' She grinned cockily at me.

'Don't get the book wet!'

'I know.' She lifted the thick leatherbound book from the stone, held it over her head and eased back down into the water. Two minutes later, she was stood at my side.

'You're brilliant! I never thought I'd say this, but go, humans!'

'Ha ha. Does your new-found appreciation for humans extend to lending me your coat, by any chance? I'm soaking.'

''Course, sorry.' I took off my coat and wrapped it around her shoulders.

'Come on, then, what are you waiting for? I'm dying to see what all this is about.' She scurried over and sat on the dry ground beneath the overhang and held the book out to me. 'You open it. Just in case it's toxic to humans or something.'

I took the Nefarium and nearly dropped it, I was so excited. Proof at last! I could show it to Dad and he'd stop the traitors and then he'd be so grateful he'd never mention Sharp Point ever again. I was saved!

I sat next to her and opened the book with a thud. I flicked to the first heavy, embossed page, trying to make sense of the old-fashioned calligraphy.

She pulled my coat tighter around her and shivered. 'What are we even looking for?'

'Not sure. Something about a wall, I guess? Or something that can give Astaroth enough power to overthrow Lucifer. Maybe it's a spell book.' But it didn't look like it. As I skimmed through, it looked more like a history book than anything.

'A history book?' she said, obviously thinking the same. 'Why would a history book be protected behind the Pond of Death?'

'I don't know.'

We leant over the book and read. And read.

'Wait, go back a page. Look.' She pressed her finger to the paper. 'The Infinite Wall – maybe that's it? Let's see, the Infinite Wall, the – no way!'

'The wall between Heaven and Hell,' I read. 'But that's ridiculous. The Other Side isn't anywhere near here. Just like Hell is in a different realm from Earth, The Other Side's in a different realm too. I mean, that's what we've always been taught. This can't be right.'

But there it was, in black and white. And it was an ancient, important-looking book. The one Morax and Baal's plot seemed to hinge on.

'Maybe it's just a book of legends, or demonic fairy stories?' she said. 'But if that's the case, why is Astaroth so desperate to find it? Anyway, where does it say this Infinite Wall is?'

I turned the page. 'At The Ends. The end of Hell. But we were always told that after The Ends there was nothing – or rather, The Great Abyss. That Hell dropped off into

136

nothingness like it does behind Pandemonium.' I frowned at the book, trying to figure it out. And then it clicked. 'God's Big Emergency!'

'Huh?'

'I overheard…a rumour that God was complaining about some big emergency in Heaven. And Baal was talking about cracks in the Wall. So maybe Morax and Baal are trying to break open the Wall for some reason – and God noticed. Maybe evil is seeping through from here into Heaven!'

'A gateway to Heaven…' she murmured, resting her chin on her hands, her dampness forgotten. 'But I don't see why Astaroth would—'

But she didn't get to finish her sentence. Morax and his men were standing across the cave, staring at us in disbelief.

14

If You Go Down to the Woods Today

'SEIZE THEM!' CRIED Morax.

Oh, *minions*.

Tommy shoved me at the overhang, said, 'Fly!' then dashed straight into the water, clutching the Nefarium.

I stared after her for a moment, wild-eyed, then flapped my wings as hard as I could and shot up into the air and over the rocks. I landed painfully on my hands and knees, kicking pebbles down onto the hellions below. They snarled up at me, unable to follow. But Morax didn't have that problem. He flexed his smooth, black wings and lifted into the air, and I scrambled to my feet and hurtled down the corridor to the fountain room.

Splashing sounds came from behind me, followed by yowls of pain.

'Take that!' yelled Tommy.

I smirked.

Dashing into the courtyard, I gave the fountain a wide

berth and flew up to the crack in the wall where we'd come in. It wasn't very wide – maybe Morax wouldn't be able to fit through. I squished through into the library, slid along the bookshelf and half fell down the ladder, before sprinting off through the stacks. Seconds later, a furious roar let me know I'd been right – Morax couldn't fit through the gap.

'Go on, then, run!' he shouted after me. 'We'll get your Bonehead girl and the book. She can't stay in the water forever!'

My stomach sank and I skidded to a halt. He was right. They'd get to Tommy eventually, she was cornered. And when they did, they'd be very, very angry.

I thunked my head against a bookshelf, denting a copy of *Tempting Humans for Fun and Profit*. I couldn't leave her there, she was my friend, and what was worse, it was all my fault she'd come. There was only one thing to do – I'd have to play the Lucifer card. If I told Morax who my dad was, he'd have to let us go. And then they'd march us back to the palace, I wouldn't have the book for proof, Dad would believe his word over mine...and I'd be in even worse trouble than before. Which hardly seemed possible.

But if I didn't, I dreaded to think what would happen to Tommy. I sighed and turned back towards Morax.

A quarter of an hour later, I was back in the cavern, a

dripping dead girl by my side and a squadron of smoking, disgruntled hellions surrounding us. Tommy *really* hadn't wanted to come out of the water. Morax stood before us, holding the Nefarium, looking like he was wondering whether to grill or fry us for breakfast.

I gulped.

'What, in the name of all that is unholy, are a demon child and a Bonehead doing down here?' he said. 'Who sent you to get this book?' He peered at me more closely. 'You look familiar, boy. What's your name?'

I bit my lip and glanced at Tommy. She wasn't going to be happy with me. But I couldn't think of anything else to do.

'Jinx D'Evil,' I said, and a couple of hellions took a step back. 'I, er, me and my serf just came to get an old book my dad needed, and then my pet bat got lost and we followed him and we didn't mean to—'

'You're *Lucifer's* son?' said Morax, taking a step closer. 'Of course, I thought you looked familiar And you say your father sent you to fetch this book?'

I suddenly realised what a stupid thing that'd been to say. He'd think Dad was onto him. 'No, no, we just came to get a book I needed for class, and we got lost...' I waved my hands vaguely around me. 'It's like a labyrinth down here.'

'And this quite ordinary schoolbook just happened to be guarded by a lake of holy water?' He tilted his head to one side and tapped on a long, curved panther fang.

'Um, no, like I said, we got lost, and I was just curious...'

Morax gave me a vicious panther smile, a smile that said, *I wonder what you taste like. If you don't stop talking I may find out.*

I stuttered to a halt.

'Well, this is unfortunate. You see, if you'd been a nobody, I might have let you go with a beating. But I really can't have you going back to the palace and telling Daddy what happened.' He snapped his finger at the captain. 'Throw this brat in the water.'

My stomach dropped out from under me.

'No, hang on, that's not going to work for the serf.'

My stomach tiptoed gingerly back to its usual position.

Morax smiled coldly. 'I know. Escort these lost children to the Frozen Forest. Discreetly. And make sure they don't return.'

'But, but – my dad will kill you if he finds out you've—'

'Precisely. Enjoy your trip!' He spun round and stalked across the cave, the Nefarium grasped firmly between his paws.

'You'll never get away with this!' I shouted after him,

furious. 'This is treason!'

He paused at the exit and smirked back at me. 'Catching on now, aren't we?'

Then he was gone.

I gazed helplessly after him, desperately wishing I could take back everything I'd said. Why had I ever thought it'd be a good idea to mention Dad? I was too stupid to live.

The circle of hellions tightened around us and I risked a peek at Tommy. She gave me the death stare to end all death stares. Oh, hellfire. Had I ever messed up this time.

Before I had the chance to think anything else, something heavy smacked me on the back of the head and the world went black.

You know how tough guys in films get hit on the head then wake up and spring straight back into action? Yeah. Not so much. I couldn't even seem to wake up all at once. I drifted in and out of darkness, my head clanging like a passing train and my mouth full of dirt. *My mouth full of dirt.* I hauled myself onto my elbows and spat. A worm came out. Gross. Spitting turned to violent retching. I batted at my tongue with the back of my hand and crawled away from the stench.

My backpack, against the odds, still clung to my shoulder. I ripped it open and found a squashed but unhurt Bruce glaring at me.

'Sorry, buddy.'

I sat on the frozen, muddy ground for several minutes, trying to get my head to stop spinning. Where was I? Eventually the whirling slowed enough for me to focus on my surroundings. The new information wasn't cheering.

Black branches scraped the dark red sky above me. Wait, branches couldn't scrape the sky...but there was a definite scraping sound. Like a knife being sharpened. Great. I scanned the forest floor until I came across a pile of clothes. Tommy. I forced myself to my feet, still woozy, the trees blurring in and out of focus.

'Tommy! Tommy, wake up!'

I staggered over and shook her shoulder. Dried blood masked half her face. 'Tommy!'

Her eyes blinked open and she sucked in a breath and tried to scramble away.

I held up my hands in front of me. 'It's OK, it's me. It's me, Jinx.'

'Uh. Oh. Where are we?' She clambered to her feet and leant against a tree trunk.

'The Frozen Forest. It's not—' The scraping noise echoed

143

out again. 'We should get out of here. Now.' I hitched my shoulder under her armpit and peered through the trees. Lights shone in the distance – somehow, we were only about twenty feet from the edge of the forest. Thank Lucifer. Or not, I remembered. We stumbled off and left the twitching branches and eerie noises behind, finding ourselves on a snow-covered plain. Phew.

'I'm surprised they didn't dump us further into the Forest, if they were trying to get rid of us,' I said. Were even hellions scared of the Frozen Forest?

She yanked her arm free and sat down on the ground. 'My head's spinning. What are those buildings over there? Is that – is that a *train*?'

'Oh, brimstone.'

It was a train. And a station. A *military* train station, swarming with hellions.

'What?'

'It's the railway station for the Infernal Express. The Fields of the Damned are on the other side. We'll have to get past it to get back to the palace.'

She looked at me like I was soft in the head. 'Are you soft in the head?'

Well, at least my deduction skills were improving. 'What do you mean? I need to get back to the palace and tell my – uh – oh.'

'Yes, *oh*,' she said, narrowing her eyes. 'Someone forgot to tell me he was the spawn of Satan, didn't he?'

'I'm not...*spawn*. But I am sorry. I didn't mean to lie. I just thought it'd freak you out.'

'No kidding. Wait till I'm distracted by being hit over the head and dumped in a creepy wood first, eh?'

'Did it work?'

'No. But anyway, we can't go back to the palace. Even if we could sneak past the hellions over there,' she pointed at the lights in the distance, 'how are we going to get in through the city gates? I bet Baal has his demons keeping an eye out for us.'

I sank to the ground beside her and put my head in my hands. She was right. 'You got a better idea, ninja girl?'

'Well, we know Grumpy Cat and his troops are going to the Infinite Wall for some reason, don't we? And even if we did make it back to the palace, you said your dad wouldn't believe you unless you had proof. So...we go to the Wall and get proof.'

It was my turn to look at her like she was soft in the head. 'Have you got any idea how far away that is? Hell's a big place, you know. It'd take us weeks to get to The Ends. And you, know, it's Hell. I may suck at Geography, but I'm pretty sure there are some nasty places between here and the Wall.'

But she was looking at me smugly. 'It wouldn't take as long – or be as scary – if we stowed away on a train, though, would it?'

'That...is a good point. But if those hellions catch us they'll take us straight back to Morax or Baal.' It was nearly dark, but dozens of horned silhouettes swarmed the station like worker ants.

'Aren't there any other stations?'

I shrugged. 'No idea. Suppose there must be. The Infernal Express was built so hellions could keep an eye on the kingdom. Since they can't fly.'

'Then let's go to the next station. It's bound to be less busy.'

The trees behind me rustled in the wind. Except it wasn't windy. 'But the only way to the next station is through the Frozen Forest.'

'So? It's only a wood. I know it's creepy, but...'

'It's not just creepy. Why do you think they dumped us there? We were lucky to get out alive.'

She grimaced. 'More Hell beasties?'

'Not exactly. Wiccas.'

'I could lie and say I know what those are, but then I'd

meet one and it'd be ten foot tall with fangs and I'd faint.'

'They aren't animals, they're Boneheads.'

'Boneheads? That sounds even scarier.'

'Oh, no – Boneheads is just our word for damned people. Like you. Wiccas are... In the old days, people didn't approve of women who tried to practise medicine. Or read books. Or do anything much, really. So they called them witches.'

She exhaled. 'Is that all? Why would they be scary, then? They're just people. Not crazy murderers or anything. And hang on, why would they be sent to Hell for practising medicine?'

'Beats me. The rules used to be a lot different centuries ago. Anyway, a lot of them got burned at the stake. Or worse. So even if they were perfectly normal people when they were alive, how sane do you think they are after dying a gruesome death then spending centuries stuck in a dark, icy forest in Hell?'

She stood up and brushed the snow off her coat. 'Meh, I bet they're just frightened. Probably sobbing in a hollow somewhere. Come on, are you a Prince of Darkness or what?'

More like a Prince of Dorkness. 'I guess.' I didn't have much choice. But I was still wondering why the hellions had dumped us only a few feet into the Forest. Were they just lazy? Or had something spooked them?

We turned away from the comforting lights and bustle of the railway station and faced the woods. They stretched far into the distance either side of us, the trees rising up like white fangs in a black mouth. There was no way round them.

She pointed down the slope. 'Look, the railway tracks go through the wood down there. If we follow them we won't get lost.'

A loud clanging rang out and I nearly bit my tongue off.

I spun round and saw the train blazing with lights. 'Must be leaving soon. Let's go.'

We trudged through the snow until we reached the place where the tracks entered the forest. I was rubbing my arms to try to keep warm when I nearly walked straight into a sign sticking out of the snow. It looked spookily like it had been written in blood.

'Abandon Hope All Ye Who Enter Here,' read Tommy. 'Always nice to have a welcome.'

I took a deep breath and stepped reluctantly back into the forest. The farther we walked, the deeper the darkness became.

I tucked her arm into mine. 'We don't want to lose each other.'

She giggled and started to skip. 'It's like *The Wizard of Oz*. Lions and tigers and bears – oh my!'

But somewhere in the distance, the eerie scraping noise had begun again. I wished she would be braver than me more quietly. I pulled her along. 'Come on, I'm freezing.'

The trees began to crowd closer together, blocking out any light from above. I could barely see where I was going, but the railway tracks underfoot kept us from wandering off. Worse, other noises filtered through the branches to join the persistent scraping sound: a muffled voice, a low growl, an unidentified thud in the distance. It was like a demonic symphony. I began to wonder if you could have a heart attack from pure fear.

A loud crack came from inches away and I froze.

'Sorry,' said Tommy, 'trod on a branch.'

I swore under my breath and shuffled on through the dirt and twigs and slush. Even Sharp Point would've been preferable to this. Suddenly something flitted past in the trees ahead.

'What was that?' whispered Tommy.

'I didn't see anything,' I lied. 'Let's just keep moving.'

She nodded, staring at her feet, walking a little faster now.

The noises seemed to multiply as we were sucked deeper into the darkness. By the time we'd been walking for half an hour, the bare, frozen woods were as loud as any tropical jungle. Any tropical jungle in Hell, that is. An eerie laugh up ahead, a shriek behind, a slithering sound to my right. Tommy trudged on, her mouth set in a grim line, pretending not to hear. Lions and tigers and bears, indeed. Chance would be a fine thing.

I tried not to think of the hellions leaving us so close to the treeline. Of course, the minute you try not to think of something, the thought runs around your brain like a toddler clashing a pair of cymbals. Had they just been spooked by the noises? Or had they run away from something? Or worse – had they *not* run away from something? Had they not been fast enough? I gulped and resisted the urge to break into a run.

There was a sharp breeze above my head. A sharp breeze not caused by any wind.

Don't look, I thought, like I was five again and hiding under the covers. *Don't look and you'll be safe*. All we had to do was put one foot in front of the other and we'd get out alive. I whispered it to myself like a mantra: *One foot in front of the other, one foot in front of the other, one...*

And then in my effort to just keep moving and not look, I tripped over a tree root and slammed into the ground, dragging Tommy with me. Lying on the slushy train tracks, for a moment I couldn't help but look up.

So did Tommy. It wasn't a good idea. She screamed.

Hanging upside down in the tree above us was a woman, her face half gone, her skin blackened and peeling. A rope around her ankles swung up into the air. She looked very dead – but her eyes were staring straight at us. Crawling backwards like a crab, I saw with horror that she wasn't the only one. Hanging from every other tree were witches. And they were all staring at us.

MEANWHILE...

Lucifer was severely disgruntled. Now that he thought about it, he couldn't remember the last time he'd felt gruntled. As if being forced to send his youngest son (who, despite all his mistakes, he was terribly fond of) to Sharp Point, Persephone going on holiday altogether too often, and God phoning him with His stupid problems wasn't enough, now He wanted to arrange a meeting. They hadn't spoken in years before His recent surprise phone call, and as for meeting face to face — it had been a millennium, at least. What could the Old Man possibly want? Was it more waffle about this Big Emergency?

To make matters worse, they had to meet on Earth, of course, because their respective realms were impossible for each other. Lucifer rarely visited the Earthly realm — all those happy humans put him in a foul mood — but it was the only alternative.

He loped warily into the Parisian café, noting the angels dotted at tables throughout, and ducked into the back room.

God was waiting at His usual table, dressed shabbily as ever in a crumpled beige mac, looking for all the world like a gently glowing Uncle Iroh. Lucifer hung his perfectly pressed black cashmere coat on a brass hook and sat down with his back to the wall.

'Good to see you,' said God, smiling his usual Isn't-the-

Universe-Mysterious-and-Enthralling smile.

Lucifer hated that smile. 'And you,' he lied.

'We appear to have a slight problem.' God took a sip of hot chocolate and leant back. 'Cracks are still appearing in the Infinite Wall. Whoever you sent to fix it can't have done a very good job, I'm afraid. I've sent angels to look at it, but they can't find anything wrong. So it must be something on your side.'

Lucifer rolled his eyes. 'Really? That's it? You've dragged me all the way to Earth just to nag me about a faulty neighbourhood fence again?'

God leant forward, and suddenly there was steel behind His kindly brown eyes. 'Need I spell out to you what would happen if the Wall were to fall?' He blinked and his eyes were gentle once more. 'You and I have come to an agreement over the years. I stay out of your way, and you stay out of mine. The humans have free will now. But if there were no Wall, our subjects might not be as inclined to keep our truce and a war could easily spread to Earth—'

Lucifer sneered. '*Earth*. That's all you ever cared about, isn't it? Earth and the humans. Those little ants, running about like brainless...ants,' he finished lamely.

God looked into his cup. 'I seem to recall there was one Earthly inhabitant you were so fond of you took her for your wife.'

Lucifer narrowed his eyes. 'That's different. Persephone is a goddess. She's special.'

'They are *all* special. Every single one of them.'

Lucifer sighed. He never won this argument. 'All right, all right, I know. I built the Wall, didn't I? I know what could happen if it wasn't there. I'll go and check on it myself.' But he couldn't help a small part of his brain, the part that always made him feel like a teenager again with his Father, mutter, *When I'm good and ready.*

'Thank you. Now, shall we have the fondue? I hear it's excellent.'

 15

The Slow Train to Hell

TOMMY GRABBED MY shoulder, her eyes white as headlights in the darkness. Without a word we leapt to our feet and ran.

All at once, the souls in the trees began to shriek in unison. 'Repent! Repent!'

A woman's voice cackled hideously as I swung past a huge spiny tree. I'd never sprinted so hard in my life. I flew over rocks and slid across patches of ice covered in spine needles. My heart hammered in my chest like it was trying to break free. I didn't blame it.

We plunged on and on, but the screaming voices only grew louder. Just as I was starting to get a stitch, the darkness began to fade to grey. We had to be getting closer to the other side of the forest. Had the witches climbed down from their trees? Were they following us? After the incident with the carousel horses I didn't dare look back to see.

I didn't have to. A woman crashed through the bushes beside us, brandishing a long knife. Blood ran from her neck and stained her white shirt. 'Killed them all! I killed

155

them all! Then myself. It was the only way.' She rushed straight at us. 'You next!'

The only thing that stopped me flapping my wings and swooping away right that second was the fear I'd fly smack into one of the burnt and twisted tree dwellers. Not even the thought of leaving Tommy behind. Yeah, I suck. I told myself she was faster than me – she'd already pulled twenty feet ahead. But I was just a coward, and a lousy demon to boot. What kind of evil demon was scared of Boneheads? I raced past the Wicca, branches dragging at my clothes. She crashed through the undergrowth behind me, shouting terrifying things. I thought I might faint from fear. Then, in the distance, I made out a dim light.

Tommy yelled at me over her shoulder. 'Come *on*!'

She crashed out of the trees into a snowy field on the other side and I followed. I didn't stop. I was all set to keep running until we hit the Infinite Wall. Tommy sped after me and dragged me to a halt.

'Let go of me!' I screamed. I wanted to get as far away as possible.

'Look,' she pointed behind us, 'they've stopped. They can't leave the forest.'

It was true. The white shirt of the crazy witch fluttered at the edge of the trees, but she wasn't coming out. I sank to the ground and clutched my head, which had started to spin again.

'It's OK,' said Tommy. 'We made it.'

'So much for harmless frightened people.' I laughed brokenly.

'I guess you're the one that ended up sobbing into a hollow.'

'Ha ha.'

We lay on the cold ground for a moment, catching our breath.

I remembered how I'd almost left her behind and felt horribly ashamed. She wouldn't have left me, I was sure of it. I was a terrible friend. 'I'm so sorry...'

'Hmph. So you should be, spawn boy, getting us dumped out here,' she said, looking angry. Then she shrugged. 'But I guess we made it in the end.' She stared into space for a moment. 'Have you ever made snow angels?'

I burst out laughing. Tommy always seemed to come up with the most random thing. I raised an eyebrow at her. 'You're asking me, a demon, if I've ever...?'

She giggled and started to brush her arms up and down in the snow. 'OK, then I'll make a snow demon. Look, this is you flying.'

I smiled and swept my arms up and down beside her.

'Me flying, all right. I managed it in Babel. Though if I tried to fly further than a few feet, I'd probably crash straight into a tree like Bruce.' I sat bolt upright. 'Bruce! Where's Bruce?'

'I think your bag's squeaking.'

'Oh, thank Hell.' I recovered a rather squashed bat from my backpack. 'Sorry, buddy, forgot you were there.' Bruce squeaked plaintively, flew in a celebratory circle and crashed into a snowdrift, leaving a small bat-shaped indentation in the snow.

'He made a snow bat!' said Tommy, hooting with laughter.

I stood up and brushed the snow off. 'Come on, let's see if we can find the next station. We're kind of exposed out here if any hellions come by.' Not that the fact that we were still really close to the Frozen Forest was creeping me out. Nope.

'Killjoy.' She got up and buried her hands in her pockets.

We crunched through the snow up a slight slope and stopped at the top to get our bearings. The train tracks snaked off into the distance, a dirty grey path in the sparkling white. But that's all there was – whiteness. There were no buildings for miles.

'Well, this is going to be an adventure,' said Tommy, in a

tone of voice that said, *kind of like a nice trip to the dentist.*

'Yup. Adventure here we come.'

But the thing about Hell is things are often not what they seem. After we'd walked for nearly an hour, the snow beneath our feet began to thin, and soon mud caked my trainers. It was getting warmer. We came to another small hill and puffed our way to the top.

'Look!' said Tommy.

I looked. 'What?' A thin mist had descended, and I couldn't see a thing. Then, for a moment, it parted, and a pointed wooden structure came into view.

'Isn't that a station?' she said.

'Yes! Look, the train tracks go right past.'

We crept down towards it, keeping a nervous eye out for hellions or fanged Hell monsters – but there was no one about. Unfortunately, there was no train either.

'Do you think we've missed it?'

I shook my head. 'At the rate we made it through the forest? Doubt it. The train doesn't go very fast, despite being called the Express. It's not exactly high-tech. Let's find somewhere comfortable to hide out and wait.'

The station was dusty and lonely-looking, like it hadn't been busy in years. White paint peeled from the wood, and if there had once been a sign, it was long gone. I opened a door marked 'Waiting Room' and a swarm of spikemoths flitted past my head.

Tommy sat on a wooden bench and squinted up at me. 'Can I ask you something? What's your dad really like?'

I sat down opposite her and shrugged. 'I dunno. He can be scary, especially when he's angry, but he's all right, really. If humans could see how googly-eyed he gets around my mum, they wouldn't think he's so bad. He'd do anything for her. Thing is, she's on holiday on Earth for half the year. Only comes back for Saturnalia.'

'What's Saturnalia?'

'It's a big party in December. You get presents and sing songs and eat lots of food.'

'Oh, like Christmas?'

I snorted. 'Kind of. Except, very much not.'

'Oh. Right. Why is your mum on Earth?'

'Persephone? It's a long story. Let's just say Dad didn't read the fine print on the pre-nup. Now she only comes home for winter. She's not a demon, so she gets sick if she spends too long down here anyway. Or that's what she says. I think she just misses the sunshine. I wish she wasn't away so much, though. I miss her.'

'At least she comes back.'

'Sorry, I didn't mean to remind you of stuff.'

Tommy stared at the floor. 'It's OK. So do you have any brothers or sisters?'

'Yeah, hundreds. Literally. 665 of them.'

Her mouth dropped open. 'Guess your dad's been around a long time. Family reunions must be a nightmare. How do you remember all their names?'

I chuckled. 'I don't. They're all thousands of years older than me, so I haven't even met half of them. They're actually half-siblings. My dad was married to someone else before my mum, a demon called Lilith. Dantalion and Morgana and Zethar still live in the palace, though, so I see them quite a lot. Dantalion's awesome, really funny and really good at being evil. I want to be like him when I grow up. Oh, I forgot, you met him in the city.'

Tommy scowled. 'Didn't seem very awesome to me.'

Ah, yes. I shut up.

We sat in silence for a moment, listening to the wind blowing outside. It was starting to get light.

She rubbed her nose. 'Why do you think Astaroth is plotting against your dad? I mean, isn't everyone scared of him?'

'I thought they were. But...to be honest, Dad hasn't been too bothered about the whole temptation business for a while now. He figures humans are pretty good at getting into trouble all by themselves. So he generally leaves them to it. Guess Astaroth and the other traitors want to put more effort into the whole spreading evil thing.'

'That doesn't sound good. For Earth, I mean. Or your dad.'

'No.'

A clanging noise floated by on the breeze. I scrambled up and opened the waiting room door. The train was coming round the bend.

'How do you know it'll stop here?' she said.

'Judging by the state of this place, I don't think it will. We

might have to run for it.'

We crossed to the other side of the tracks and hid behind a thorny clump of bushes. The long train started to chug past. Tommy crouched down further at the sight of the hellion in the driver's cab. It was going slowly, but it didn't seem to be stopping.

I spotted an open door three boxcars away. 'There!'

I bolted alongside the train, grabbed the door handle, and swung up, landing face-first on the floor. Ow. I reached back to help Tommy but she gripped the ledge and flipped nimbly up onto the rattling train alongside me.

'Smooth.'

She gave a little bow. 'Benefits of being a circus kid. Though if I'd known acrobatics would come in handy for Hell one day, I'd have trained a lot harder.'

Safely inside, I let Bruce out and pulled the door almost closed. Then we lay down, using our coats for pillows, and fell instantly asleep.

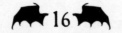

How Grim Was My Valley

SOMETHING ABOUT THE slow thrumming of the train meant I slept like a sloth in a hammock. When I woke up I felt ready to take on the world. We'd escaped the Frozen Forest and managed to hitch a ride on the Infernal Express. Things weren't going so badly. In a few days we'd be at The Ends and then...my stomach rumbled loudly. That reminded me. I hadn't eaten in nearly a day. I dug a grimberry cupcake out of my bag and went to peer out of the door.

A snuffling sound came from behind me.

'Hey, Tommy.'

'Heyurgh?' She rubbed her eyes and crawled over to look out of the door – just in time to see another signpost declaring 'Abandon Hope All Ye Who Enter Here!' blur past.

Great. We could do without another bunch of creepy dead people trying to kill us. Then again, maybe they just put those signs up everywhere in Outer Hell to freak out the Boneheads.

She pushed the door open a little wider. 'Do you know what land is south of the Frozen Forest?'

'Um. I never was very good at Geography. Plus I've never actually been out here, remember? Let's see, there are the Fields of the Damned for the lesser sinners. Then the Frozen Forest with the witches. Before The Ends are the Nex Mountains, where the worst humans are sent – the murderers – and in between is...Thieves' Canyon, I think?'

'That's not a canyon.'

She was right. The snow and mud had disappeared overnight, and outside was a lush green valley backed by rolling hills. The sky was the colour of dried blood, and swirling grey fog dipped down into the fields.

'It'll come to me,' I said, yawning. 'Cupcake?'

'No thanks, I'm all right. Plus, who knows when we'll be able to get food again. You'd better keep it for yourself.'

'OK, thanks.' I dangled my legs out of the shuddering box car and watched a flock of gamrins – the two-headed vultures Tommy had been so spooked by – skim by. Which gave me an idea. I swung round and emptied the contents of my backpack onto the floor. Two comics, three cupcakes, a half-empty bottle of banana milk and...a pen.

'Taking inventory?' she asked.

'Nope. Sending a message in a bottle.'

'Huh?'

'We might not be able to get back into the city, but I bet

a small bat could. I'm going to tie a note to Bruce and send him to the palace. I'm pretty sure he can find his way home.'

'Won't it be hard to get a message to your dad?'

'Yes. Which is why I'm going to send it to Loiter.'

'Loiter?'

'The Patron Demon of Sloth. He's my friend. He'll help us.'

'Sloth? That's laziness, right?'

'Yes, and—'

She burst out laughing.

'What?'

'Really? Out of all the scary, evil, terrifying demons you could have had to call on for help, you have the patron saint of laziness?'

I crossed my arms, offended. 'Demon, not saint. And Loiter might not be terrifyingly evil, but that's why he's my friend. And why he'll help us.'

She bit her lips together, but her eyes glittered with mirth. 'OK, I'm sorry.'

I flicked open one of the comics to a page showing Spider-Man and Deadpool and waved it at her.

'See? Even superheroes need friends.'

Tommy raised an eyebrow. 'They're insulting each other.'

'That's what best friends do, numb brain.'

Tommy smirked. 'Dork breath.'

'Zombie girl.'

'Spawn of Satan.'

'Haha.' I scribbled a message to Loiter over the top of the panel. The words 'urgent' and 'help' featured prominently. I hoped he was back from Texas. He would know what to do. Then I tied it around Bruce's leg with the string from the cake package and gave him a light shove into the air.

'How do you know Bruce won't get lost? Or fly around a bit and come back to us?'

I didn't.

He fluttered off in the direction of Pandemonium and I watched him go, hoping the lure of Pop Rocks would lead him back to my bedroom.

'The fate of the realm depends on you!' I yelled after him. 'No pressure!'

The train headed downhill, deeper and deeper into the valley. Scents of fresh grass and rain wafted through the air, like an Earthly spring, making me uneasy. Something was off about this place. No, not uneasy – sad. Not miserable, just a little drip drip drip of discomfort at the back of my mind, like a broken tap.

Tommy sniffed. 'This reminds me of the countryside where the circus was the day...the day my mum abandoned me. The birds were singing and the sun was shining but...' Her face grew pale, freckles standing out sharply like a game of join-the-dots.

I wasn't sure what to say, so I didn't say anything. Sometimes people just want to be listened to, anyway.

'When it happened, you know...I was too young to understand she was gone for good. She left and I remember waving goodbye, thinking she'd be back the next day. And then I thought she'd be back the day after that, or the next day. I waited and waited and she never...I was only five, how could she do that? I can't even remember her face.

Why, why would she leave me with my uncle like that?' She started to sob, fat tears rolling down her cheeks.

I scooted closer and put an arm round her. 'I'm so sorry.'

'No, I'm sorry, forget it. I miss Sayonara more than her, to be honest. She was the one who looked after me.' She brushed the tears roughly off her face. 'I just feel so sad all of a sudden, like a light's gone out inside me.'

Like a... 'That's it!' I said, excited for a nanosecond.

'What's it?'

'I know where we are. We're in the Valley of Despair! That's why you're feeling like this.'

'Oh. That doesn't make me feel much better, to be honest. What about you, doesn't it work on you?'

I thought about how much I missed Mum, and how I didn't have a single friend at school. Most of all, I thought about how much Dad must hate me if he was willing to send me to Sharp Point. 'Oh yeah, it works on me.'

'What are you sad about? Please, help me stop thinking about Mum.'

I unhooked my arm from her back and leant against the rattling box car wall. 'My dad,' I said. 'I know you laughed at me before, but it's true – all I want is for him to be proud of me. I mean, he's the Prince of Darkness, a legend, the coolest bad guy ever. How am I supposed to live up to that?

169

Especially when I suck at being evil.'

'Maybe by travelling all the way to The Ends to get proof of Astaroth's plans.'

I sighed. 'Yeah, if trying to do that doesn't get us killed first.'

We sat in gloomy silence for a moment. Talking wasn't helping. The more I talked, the more misery flowed through me like a bone-chilling grey fog.

She cocked her head. 'Maybe you aren't meant to be evil. Maybe you're meant for other things.'

'Like what? What else is there? I'm a demon. Being evil is what we do.'

'I don't know, what if...'

I leapt to my feet. 'The fog!'

'What about it?'

A grey fog of misery. I leant against the open door and shoved. It wouldn't budge. 'Help me shut this!'

'Why – oh. You think it's the fog?'

'I don't know, but I don't think it's helping.'

'There's a catch on the floor.' She kicked it lightly with her toe and the door flew shut with a loud bang, leaving us in darkness.

As my eyes grew used to it, I noticed pinpricks of daylight coming from all over. I sat back down on the floor.

'Do you feel any better?' asked Tommy.

'No. But give it time. Maybe we have to get it out of our systems first, like food poisoning or something. What about you?'

'A bit. But that might just be from talking to you. Sayonara once told me the best cure for being sad is trying to cheer someone else up.' She managed a watery smile. 'You should've seen me when I first learned to throw knives. I was *awful*. I cut through the Bearded Lady's washing line so many times she had to make one from wire. One time I scalped a passing clown.'

I snorted.

'But Sayonara was so patient. She never gave up on me.' She leant against the wall and crossed her arms. 'You know, I had a thought.'

'Only one?'

She rolled her eyes. 'You're Lucifer's six hundred and sixty-sixth child. Number 666?'

'And?'

'Well, isn't 666, like, an important number to your dad? I heard that once. So maybe that's why you're better at being good than being bad. Maybe there's a reason you are like you are.'

The last of my misery vanished. 'You think I'm supposed

to be like this? On purpose? Like I'm...destined or something?'

She shrugged. 'Could be. Could be a thing.'

'I think that's...about as likely as Loiter running a marathon.' I burst out laughing. 'Besides, 666 is an Evil number, not a Good one. But thanks for the thought. Maybe I can be Captain Destiny now, instead of Captain Doom.'

She grinned. 'You never know. Captain Destiny has a nice ring to it. So how long do you think it'll take the train to get through this Valley of Despair, then?'

I shut my eyes and tried to picture the map of Hell we'd studied in school. It didn't work. 'I'm sorry, I don't know. Why don't we go back to sleep for a bit? Maybe the worst'll be over by the time we wake up.'

'OK. All this rocking does make me sleepy. Maybe the next stop'll be the Land of Ice Cream and Chocolate.'

Somehow I doubted it.

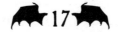 17

The Lie of Blue Skies

WHEN I WOKE up I saw stars.

Where was I? I rubbed my eyes. The gentle clattering of the train brought me back to earth. No, not stars. Bright pinpricks of sunshine streaming through the holes and cracks in the boxcar. And the musty smell of hot dust. That was odd.

'Tommy?'

She stretched her whole body like a cat and got up from the floor. 'I feel so much better. Do you think it's safe to open the door?'

'We won't know till we try.' I heaved the heavy iron door open a cautious few inches, and was blinded by bright sunlight. 'Ugh. *Sunshine?*'

'What a beautiful day! Looks we've left the Valley behind.' She leant out of the door and grinned. 'Hey, that looks like blue sky over there!'

We had definitely left the Valley behind. The train was now chugging slowly – slower than before, it seemed to me – through a desert-like landscape. A shimmering heat haze hovered above golden sand dunes dotted with green cacti, making everything slightly out-of-focus, like I was looking at it through the wrong side of a lens.

'That's funny,' I said. 'I've never seen blue sky in Hell before.' I definitely didn't take after Mum when it came to sunshine and blue skies. They creeped me out. 'Anyway, thank Lucifer we're out of the Valley, that was awful.'

She lifted her freckled face to the sun, soaking in the warmth. 'Yeah. I feel like I've remembered how to smile. This is almost like being back on Earth again.'

Give me Hell's red skies any day, I thought, but I didn't want to spoil it for her. At the back of my mind, I couldn't help wondering if we'd missed another 'Abandon All Hope' sign.

Tommy yawned. 'You ever been to Earth?'

'A few times. Like when I went to stay with my private tutors. Although those visits didn't end well.' I smirked at the memory of Blackbeard's beach wedding. 'And on school trips.'

'You went on school trips to Earth?'

'Yeah, to show us how awful humans are, and to help us decide what kind of career we want when we grow up.'

She squinted at me. 'Career?'

'You know, whether we want to lead humans into

temptation, or help speed up global warming, or maybe go into science and create new insect species that destroy crops. That kind of thing.'

'And did it help you decide?'

'No. Kind of had the opposite effect, actually. I rather liked Earth. You can't get grape Slush Puppy in Hell. Or Mario Kart.'

Tommy grinned.

'I mean, all those green trees and blue skies and sunlit oceans aren't really my thing,' I said. 'Though I went to one place that had black sand beaches, which was cool. But the cities are brilliant. They just have this energy, you know? All those skyscrapers and shops and buzzing crowds, and the pollution makes it smell like home.'

She burst out laughing. 'You would like that. You demons are so weird. So how do you get there, anyway? I mean, from here? Do you beam up, like in a sci-fi movie?'

'No – originally, every country had a hidden portal to Hell, although with the way the world's changed over the millennia, some have more than one now and some don't have any. Anyway, when I leave Hell, I go into a big waiting room beneath the palace. There are a lot of forms to fill in and then they crank up this old machine which looks like two giant brass wheels. They set one wheel to a certain place on Earth, and the other to a certain period in time. Then I go through the door, and I'm in Transylvania in 1843 or wherever.'

She stared at me like I'd just told her unicorns were real. 'That is so cool! How do you get home again?'

'Back out through the portal. It's usually some old disused cave or something. The portals are invisible to humans – you wouldn't know it's there unless you're a demon. You go through some crack in a rock or whatever, and you'll be in a waiting room again. Then someone on the other side opens the door and lets you back into Hell.'

'Wow.'

'But what you were saying about beaming up – the very oldest demons, like my dad and Loiter, can do that. So you see Loiter isn't as useless as you thought.'

'Uh oh. Does that mean Astaroth can too?'

I scratched my head. 'I don't think so. He wasn't my dad's original right-hand man – they fell out. I think he's only been around for a few thousand years.'

'What about – hang on, is that a woman over there?'

I looked where she was pointing. Walking over the sand dunes towards the train was, in fact, a Bonehead woman. Who was waving at us.

'What in Dad's name?' I said, startled.

The woman began to run, still waving.

'Do you think she needs our help?' said Tommy. 'Maybe...'

The woman was now close enough to see her long black hair and blue jeans. She was young, maybe twenty. There was no blackened skin or any other sign of violent death. She seemed...normal. But what was she doing out here, alone?

'We can't get off the train,' I said. 'What if we can't get back on again?'

But Tommy wasn't listening – she was staring, slack-jawed, at the woman, like she didn't know whether to laugh or cry. And then, without a word, she jumped out of the train. She landed in a neat roll in the sand, leapt to her feet, and yelled, 'Sayonara!'

It was my turn to stare slack-jawed. Her friend from the circus? That made no sense. She was still alive. Or was supposed to be. I swore loudly. If we left the train behind it'd take us forever to get to The Ends. But if I didn't jump now I was going to lose Tommy. I grabbed my backpack and dived out into the desert after her.

And that's when things really started to get weird.

I ran after Tommy, who was running towards the woman. The woman had stopped waving and running and was now walking slowly towards Tommy. But the strange thing was, she didn't seem to be getting any closer. Suddenly she spoke.

'My little ninja!'

'Sayonara? Is that really you? What are you doing here?'

'Oh, Tommy, I've missed you so much, come here.' She held out her hands towards her.

They were still several yards apart. Then, before my eyes, Tommy began to sink into the sand.

'Tommy!' I raced towards her and skidded to a stop. Because standing right in front of me was my dad.

'Dad? Did you get my message? What's happening?'

'Yes, son, I got your message. I'm sending demons after Astaroth right now. It's all going to be OK.'

I stared at him. He wasn't angry. He believed me, he—

'Jinx, help!' I spun round. Tommy was now up to her waist in what was clearly quicksand. Sayonara hovered in the distance, making no move towards her.

'Dad, I have to help my friend!'

His brow furrowed, as if I were a puzzle he didn't understand. 'A Bonehead? Don't be silly, son. The damned get what they deserve in Hell. Come on, let's go home now.'

'I – I can't, I have to rescue her.' I couldn't believe I was disobeying him. Again. Just when he was finally happy with me. I hesitated, wanting more than anything to keep him happy, to go home with him, to be the good son. Wait...*son*? Dad never called me son. And I hadn't mentioned Astaroth in my message, since I couldn't be sure he was the ringleader. The only names I'd given were Baal's and Morax's.

'You're not real,' I said with a gasp.

'Don't be silly, Jinx, of course I am, I...' He stood before me, barring my way.

'Jinx! Sayonara! Please help!' Tommy was slapping at the sand as it sucked at her shoulders. Her friend still hadn't moved a muscle.

I dashed past Dad, or whatever he was, flapped my wings and lifted into the baking hot air. I hovered unsteadily above Tommy. 'Give me your hands!'

She threw her arms up and I grabbed onto them and pulled. And pulled. She rose a few inches then lost her grip and fell back into the quicksand. I suddenly remembered what she'd told me, back in the Fields of the Damned. If I didn't get her out, she'd be doomed to drown in the quicksand over and over for eternity. The thought made me break out in a cold sweat. I wobbled over her, concentrating as hard as I could on my flying. I could do it, I was born to fly, all I had to do was *concentrate*.

I grasped her round the wrists and heaved, keeping my fluttering slow and steady as I rose into the air. Suddenly

there was a revolting sucking sound like a sea monster belching and she shot up out of the quicksand like an earthworm. I jerked backwards with her dangling below and we crashed into a dune in a tangle of arms and legs.

She spat out a mouthful of sand. 'You so need to work on your flying skills.'

'Sorry I didn't have a white horse handy to rescue you.'

'I'm kidding.' She gave me a hug. 'Thank you, thank you, thank you. You saved my life.' Her face dropped. 'I don't

180

understand, Sayonara just stood there...'

We spun round. The heat haze winked at us over the bare sands. Totally, completely bare. There was no one there. Not Tommy's friend, not my dad. There never had been. It had all been a trick, a mirage.

A light went off in my head. 'The Desert of Deception.'

'Huh?'

'*That's* what this place is, I remember now. It's one of the most dangerous places in Hell, because you never know what's real and what isn't.'

Her face crumpled like she'd been slapped. 'Sayonara...'

'Wasn't really here. I'm so sorry.'

She took a deep breath. 'No, no, it's OK. It's good. If she was here, that'd mean she was dead. I'd never want that.'

But her watery eyes looked longingly at the place where her friend had been standing.

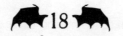

Guess Who's Coming For Dinner

I SHOOK THE sand off my clothes and started to laugh. Tommy was covered from head to toe in sludge. 'You look like a lump of cookie dough that's about to go in the oven.'

She wrestled with her filthy duffel coat for a second, then pulled out a muddy throwing star and waved it at me. 'Not. Another. Word.'

I smirked. 'Hey, I don't know what you're complaining about. At least you don't need to eat or drink.' I took the last of the banana milk from my bag and swallowed it gratefully. 'I wish I didn't. This place is making me really thirsty. Come on, let's get out of here.'

We jogged off through the sand towards the tracks. But the train was long gone.

I ran a hand through my hair. 'Well, that sucks. It was going so slowly, I thought we might be able to catch up with it.'

'Maybe it went through the desert more slowly than

usual on purpose. To trick us.'

'Yeah. Looks like we're going to have to do it on foot. At least we have the tracks to follow. Let's hope the Desert isn't too big.'

But three hours' slow, sweaty, traipsing later, there was still no end in sight. Nothing but sand, the odd pebble and more sand. Even the cacti had vanished. I glared at the ugly Earth-like blue sky and sun, and began to wonder if demons could get sunstroke.

'Shouldn't you be immune to heat?' asked Tommy. 'I mean, you're immune to hellfire, right?'

'Yeah, and brimstone. But not sunshine. We don't normally get any in Hell, but I guess the Desert plays by its own rules.' I was so going to have a word with Dad about that.

Dad. I remembered the mirage. Of course it'd been too good to be true. Like Dad would've forgiven me for running away so easily, even if he did find out about the plot. He'd still be angry at me for disobeying him. Well, there was no point worrying about that now. I concentrated on putting one foot in front of the other and getting out of the sweltering heat.

After another hour, we stopped to rest. Tommy's face was red from the exertion and the fake sun. I longed for swirling red mist.

'Get any more burnt and you'll blend right in with us demons,' I said with a grin, trying to lighten the atmosphere.

'Very funny. Are you OK? You must be really thirsty.'

I was. My throat was sore from swallowing grains of sand and I'd started to have visions of lapping pools of water that I hadn't told Tommy about. I knew they weren't real.

'I'll live.' I hoped.

We stood up again and continued our trek. The sun beat down relentlessly and all I could do was think of water. Clear, crisp, icy cold water. Running down my throat and over my head. I plodded on, but I was dizzy with longing. My head throbbed like a herd of tiny were-rhinos were stabbing my skull from the inside. Then red spots began to float in front of my eyes. I stopped and squinted. The world was going fuzzy at the edges. 'Tommy, uh...' And then it faded away completely.

I came round to Tommy shaking me. 'Huh?' I said eloquently.

'You fainted. How many fingers am I holding up?' She held up her thumb.

I gave her a wan smile and raised myself gingerly

onto my knees.

'Don't get up,' she said, 'let's camp here for the night. It's getting dark anyway.'

I liked that plan. I lay back down in the sand.

Tommy sat down across from me and leant back on her elbows.

For a while, we just stared up at the blue-black sky in silence.

'It wasn't all bad in the circus, you know,' she said quietly.

'No?'

'When you step out into the ring, and smell the lions and elephants and sawdust and popcorn, and feel the hot lights on you, and the music starts and the audience leans forward in anticipation...there's this electricity. Then when you've done your part of the show and the applause practically lifts the roof off the big top... It's kind of magical.'

She held up a handful of sand and let it run through her fingers. 'Once, I even got into the newspaper. "Ten-year-old knife-throwing prodigy", they called me, and they took my picture and asked me...'

But my eyelids were growing heavier and heavier. I drifted back into unconsciousness.

I dreamed I was flying over the palace. I'd never flown that high before and for a moment I was terrified, but then I realised how smoothly I was moving, and relaxed. I soared over the shiny black turrets of Darkangel Palace, dipping and swooping like a bird. Demons ran around far below like red ants, and I peered into windows and watched serfs preparing dinner and librarians stacking books. An enormous sense of calm came over me. Somehow I knew it was a dream, but all the same, I felt as though when I woke up I would be able to fly like this. It had always been inside me, I just hadn't— An ear-splitting screech shook me to the core and I turned to see a monstrous eagle bearing down on me. I screamed.

'Jinx! Jinx! Wake up!'

I thrashed my way back awake, happy to leave the monstrous bird behind. But my relief was short-lived. High in the dark blue sky, a flock of two-headed gamrins was circling – and they looked like they had dinner on their minds.

'Oh, brimstone.' I shoved myself groggily to my feet, and scanned the desert. Flat sand stretched unhelpfully away on all sides. There was nowhere to hide.

The gamrins swooped this way and that on their wide grey wings, razor-sharp orange beaks snapping at us.

'Hell vultures,' said Tommy. 'Why did it have to be Hell vultures?' She pulled out a throwing star and hurled it at them, but they dodged it easily and continued to circle, cawing for blood.

'They don't seem to be coming any closer,' she said. 'Let's—'

A sharp pain rocketed through my head and I fell to my knees. I flapped at the bird that had dive-bombed me, shrieking.

'Stop moving,' said Tommy, 'I can't hit it if you – ow!'

All at once we were inside a maelstrom of beaks and feathers and claws. I punched and kicked and slapped at the air around me, but the gamrins were huge and everywhere. In seconds, I was curled into a ball, hands bleeding and sore, trying desperately to protect my face and eyes. After coming this far, we were going to be pecked to death by a flock of birds. I would've screamed with frustration if I hadn't been too busy yelling in pain.

And then came the fire.

Heat rushed by my head, and a gamrin squealed in my ear. All at once, the storm of claws and beaks lifted and I risked a peek through my hands: birds were cartwheeling through the air, flaming like phoenixes. I was so relieved that the biting and scratching had stopped, at first I didn't understand. Then I saw it: a figure in the purple pre-dawn, blasting fire at the birds, roasting every last one.

My head slumped in relief, then snapped back up. Was this another mirage? The last vision of a dying demon? I rolled onto my hands and knees. Nope, not dead. Too sore to be dead. Blood dripped into my eyes and I wiped it away to see the last of the gamrins fall to earth, smelling distractingly like Sinday roast. The figure in the distance dropped its arms and walked towards me. It was...a sloth.

'Loiter?'

'Hello, Jinx. Got yourself into a bit of a tight spot, I see.'

I couldn't believe it. 'Are you really real?'

He smiled. 'I really am.'

I ran and flung my arms round him.

'Steady on, old chap, don't crease the fur.'

'You're actually here. Wait, tell me something only you would know.'

He raised an eyebrow. 'Trouble with mirages, eh? Well, I know a mirage couldn't do *that*.' He waved at the blackened carcasses dotting the landscape. 'Also, I know it was you who gave the school dragon the wrong food last term, and accidentally turned him into a very disgruntled bunny rabbit.'

I grinned sheepishly. 'Wow, am I glad to see you. So Bruce delivered the message?'

'Well, he didn't so much as deliver the message as I found

188

him with his head stuck in a packet of Pop Rocks in your bedroom, weak from exhaustion, but yes. Quite a mess you've got yourself into, eh? And who's this?' He waved at Tommy, who was standing, scratched and incredulous, staring at him.

'This is Tommy, yes, I know she's a Bonehead but she's my friend, and she's been helping me to...'

He waved off my excuses. 'Don't worry about it.' He peered at Tommy. 'You look strangely familiar. Don't suppose we've met before, have we?'

'I don't think so. Pretty sure I'd remember a killer sloth.'

He chuckled. 'No, no, my mistake. Anyway, pleased to meet you, Tommy.' He held his paw out politely.

'This...is not a mirage, right?' she said to me.

'No, this is Loiter.'

She shook his long claws gingerly. 'Pleased to meet you. Nice timing with the bringing-of-fiery-death, appreciate it.'

'I didn't even know you could do that,' I said.

He looked down at his paws, which were still smoking a little. 'Well, it's been a while since I've got into a fight, that's for sure. Glad to see I haven't lost my touch.' He rootled around in his fur and thrust a bottle of water at me. 'You look like you need this.'

I could have kissed him. Except, you know, sloth-breath.

I gulped the water down in seconds. I'd never tasted anything so sweet. It was like being brought back from the dead.

Loiter scratched his nose. 'Now, we've got a lot of catching up to do, and apparently, a revolution to quell. So let's go somewhere comfy and discuss our plans.'

'Somewhere...comfy?' said Tommy, raising an eyebrow. There was nothing but sand for miles.

He waved a paw nonchalantly. 'I have some friends nearby. Hang on a minute, and I'll go and fetch us some transport.' He vanished in a blur of amber light.

Tommy looked like she was going to cry. 'So he was just a mirage.'

I stared at the pawprints in the sand, and felt the water swishing round in my belly. 'Oh no, he was real. We're going to be OK now. It's all going to be OK.'

She sank onto the ground and propped her chin on her hands. 'I really hope you're right.'

For once, I was. Just as the sun was peeking over the horizon, a peculiar rumbling rang out in the distance. The rumbling turned into a sand storm, and the sand storm turned into a trio of riders on horseback. Well, not *horse*back, strictly speaking.

'What are those?' said Tommy, backing away.

'Kravrons. It's the cavalry!'

Loiter pulled up in front of us riding a black, scaly, horse-like beast with fiery red eyes, and pulling two more beside him.

'I hope you know how to ride,' he said.

Tommy grabbed my arm. 'What are those things?'

Loiter patted his kravron fondly. 'This is Edna, please don't call her a thing, she'll get upset. They're lovely animals, there's no need to be afraid.'

'They're Hell's version of horses,' I said. I climbed up

into the saddle of the nearest one. 'Who's this?'

'Alfred,' said Loiter. He beckoned Tommy over and handed her the reins to the third beast. 'And this is Doris. Hop on up, young lady.'

Tommy stared at the reins with a look on her face like she'd jumped out of an aeroplane and found a hole in her parachute. She started to back away, but Doris licked her hand, and whinnied softly at her.

'See?' I said. 'Very friendly.' I stroked Alfred's leathery mane.

'I hate you.' Tommy took a deep breath and leapt up into the saddle.

'Right, hi ho, Silver,' said Loiter.

'But where did you get these?' I asked. 'And where are we going?'

'To see an old friend of mine called Sarika.' He smiled. 'You might know her better as the Bandit Queen.'

19

Thick As Thieves

'THE BANDIT QUEEN?' hissed Tommy as we rode along behind Loiter. 'How does that sound like a good idea?'

I wasn't sure it did. Sarika Amra. Wow. We'd learned about her in History – a legendary Indian robber who'd preyed on the British upper classes during the Raj. In India, she was a folk hero, kind of like Robin Hood, because she'd shared some of her loot with the poor. But I still wasn't sure if walking into the lair of a fearless Bonehead bandit was exactly a smart move.

I put on a brave face. 'She's only a robber. Otherwise she'd be in the Nex Mountains, with the murderers. Let's just see what happens. I trust Loiter, and you should too.'

'Hmph. I guess he saved my life, so I'll give him the benefit of the doubt.' But she didn't look happy about it.

After a while, the sand began to harden into red rock, the flat dunes twisted and turned into gulleys and tors, and soon the desert had vanished altogether and we were in what could only be Thieves' Canyon. And with the end of deception, came the end of blue skies...and the sun. I'd never been so relieved to see the swirling marmalade skies of Hell. My head was throbbing, and I was still so thirsty I wanted to dive into a swimming pool and then drink it. Sadly, I doubted a rough-and-tumble robbers' camp would have a swanky recreation area.

Loiter, in the lead, had reached the top of a rocky bluff. 'Here we are!' he said, turning and smiling at us. 'Welcome to Larceny.'

I trotted up next to him. And stared.

Tommy pulled Doris up beside me. 'That's...not what I was expecting.'

There was no dusty, ragged, bandit hideout to be seen. Instead, a pretty little village of whitewashed houses and tidy streets spread out before us.

Loiter grinned and cantered off down the slope and we followed, eyes wide.

'I thought Pandemonium was the only town in Hell,' said Tommy.

So had I. 'Wow. Loiter, how come...?'

'This place exists? Well, they are a bunch of thieves. Dare say they've robbed the Infernal Express a few times. Don't tell your father.'

We skidded to the bottom of the slope and trotted gently down the high street, past dressmakers and grocery stores with colourful awnings, and houses with neatly brushed front steps. I wasn't sure whether to be more shocked at the existence of the town or that Loiter seemed to be friendly with a bunch of Boneheads.

He slid off his kravron, tied the reins to a fence, and beckoned us into a saloon bar that looked like something out of the Wild West, only without the mud and sawdust. We followed him through the swinging wooden doors and sat at a table.

'Drink?' said Loiter.

'I'm guessing they don't have banana milk. Can I have the biggest glass of water you can find?' I said.

'I'm OK, thanks,' said Tommy, gazing up at a chandelier that appeared to be made of reshaped railway tracks.

Loiter loped off to the bar, which was fashioned from rusty boxcar siding, past a table where a group of Boneheads sat playing poker. In the middle sat a woman in a brightly coloured sari and a worn leather jacket, with a huge pile of money in front of her. Sharp brown eyes peered from beneath the brim of a fedora, and a faded scar zigzagged across her face.

I nudged Tommy. 'That's her,' I whispered. 'The Bandit Queen. I recognise her from my textbooks.'

Loiter dipped down and said something in Sarika's ear

as he returned, and she nodded. He sat back at our table and I grabbed the dripping glass of water and downed it in one long swallow. I still felt wobbly. I folded my arms on the table and rested my head on them.

'Better? Sarika will join us in a moment. In the meantime, I think you'd better tell me everything you two troublemakers have been up to. From the beginning.'

So we did.

When I got to the part about the Nefarium, Loiter held up a paw. 'So Morax knows the secret of the Infinite Wall? That's unfortunate. Jolly poor security, leaving the book lying around like that.'

I gaped at him. 'You knew Heaven was on the other side? Why didn't you tell me? I thought it was just a fairy tale.'

He shrugged. 'You never asked. Go on.'

'So Astaroth and the other traitors want to take over from Dad. Seems like they think Dad isn't putting enough effort into spreading evil on Earth, or something.'

'I think the humans do a pretty good job of that on their own, to be honest,' said Loiter.

'Yeah, I think that's what Dad thinks. Anyway – the rebels want to take over from Dad, but I don't know why they think breaking through the Wall will help them do that.'

Loiter tilted his head thoughtfully. 'Hmm, I think I

might. I bet they're trying to start another war between Heaven and Hell. Baal is the Chief of Staff, after all. If all the armies were ranged under his command for a war, it'd be the easiest time to take over from Lucifer.'

'And of course Lucifer wouldn't know they were behind the Wall cracking open,' said Tommy. 'So he'd send them off with all the armies to fight...and then they'd use his own soldiers against him.'

'Maybe they don't even really want a war,' I said. 'Maybe it's just an excuse.'

Loiter took a sip of his cocktail. 'You may be right. Are you certain it's Astaroth who's behind all this?'

'No,' I admitted. 'He just...'

'Looks like he might rip you open and play the xylophone on your ribs?' he said.

'Well, um, yes.'

'Just because you don't like the way he looks doesn't make him a traitor.' He gave me a stern look.

I felt my cheeks grow warm. 'It isn't just that. He's also Dad's second-in-command. It would make sense if it was him.'

'Hmm, fair point. All the same, we cannot condemn him yet, not without proof.'

'What about Lucifer?' said Tommy.

'Yeah, where's my dad?'

'Ah. Slight problem. He's not here.'

I froze. 'What do you mean, not here? Is he OK? Has Astaroth – or whoever – kidnapped him?'

'No, don't worry. His secretary told me he's gone away for a short while. To Earth.'

My eyes nearly bugged out of my head. '*Earth?* But he hates Earth, he hardly ever goes there unless...'

'Unless he has a VIP meeting.'

'Of course.'

Tommy scowled at us. 'Will you two stop speaking in code? What VIP meeting?'

'A meeting with the Other Side,' said Loiter.

'You mean God?' she said with a gasp. 'They meet up – on Earth?'

Loiter waved his glass nonchalantly. 'Of course, my dear, they couldn't very well meet in each other's domains, now could they?'

I tried to digest this. Part of me had been dreading seeing Dad again, with all the trouble I'd be in. But it was *Dad*, and I knew he'd fix this mess somehow – he always did. What were we supposed to do without him? My head began to throb again. 'Maybe that was part of their plan? Maybe they knew Dad would have to go to a VIP meeting on Earth, and that would get him out of the way for a while?'

Loiter nodded. 'Could be.'

'So if Dad's not coming, what do we do? How are we supposed to stop an army on our own? Is anyone else coming to help?'

Loiter tapped a claw on the table. 'I'm afraid not, at least not yet. With Baal and Morax mixed up in this, I wasn't sure who to trust. Anyone could be in on it. So I didn't dare talk to anyone at the palace. Until your father returns, it's up to us – we need to get to The Ends and try to keep the Wall in one piece.'

There was a low screech as Sarika pulled out a chair and sat down next to me. She slapped Loiter on the back. 'Hello, old friend, good to see you.'

'And you, my dear.'

'How do you – I mean, if it isn't rude – but how do you two know each other?' I stuttered.

The Bandit Queen smiled warmly, displaying a mouthful of gold fillings. 'My friend here may have helped me with sending a few rich Englishmen to sleep, back in the day. So I could relieve them of their belongings without bloodshed. I do not enjoy the sight of blood. But I do so enjoy a full treasure chest.'

Tommy gazed at her like she'd just discovered her new heroine.

Loiter clapped his paws together. 'Right, this is the plan. When your father is at a VIP meeting, the location is hidden. Nonetheless, I do know a couple of spots where they've met before. So I'm going to pop over to Earth and have a look for him.'

'What if you can't find him?' I said.

'Well, either way, he should return to Hell soon. In the meantime, Sarika here is kindly going to escort you to the edge of the Canyon.'

'I'm afraid we cannot leave Thieves' Canyon,' she said, 'or we would come with you to The Ends.'

'Yes. Pity,' said Loiter. 'So you two are going to have to nip through the Caves of Wrath and head on over to Nex by yourselves. Then—'

'*Nip through?*' I said, the throbbing in my head turning into a fully fledged drum solo. 'Nip through underground caves filled with angry hellbeasts and a mountain range crawling with murderers? On our own? *That's* your great plan?'

'Now, now, you really needn't worry. I happen to know that Tafrac, the Patron Demon of Wrath, isn't home right now. I believe he's down on Earth, busy making people angry with a new scheme, something to do with website comments.'

'But what about Nex?' asked Tommy. 'Jinx told me it was full of murderers.'

'Yes, a rather unsavoury place, I'm afraid. But—'

'Excuse me, um, Queen,' interrupted Tommy.

'Yes, my dear?'

Tommy tugged a throwing star out of her pocket. 'I don't suppose you have any more of these, do you?'

Sarika's eyebrows nearly shot off the top of her head. 'Well, child, aren't you full of surprises? Come with me when we're done here, and I'll see what I can do.'

Loiter chuckled. 'It seems the denizens of Nex should be worried about *you*, young lady. Nonetheless, as I was saying, I should be back in time to escort you both through the mountains.'

I jumped to my feet, more in irritation at Loiter seeing Tommy as my bodyguard than his nonchalant tone. '*Should?*'

'*Will* be. Now...'

But jumping to my feet hadn't been a good idea. My head swam, and the room began to spin. I grabbed for the table and missed. Somewhere in the distance, I felt pain, and then I felt nothing.

I opened my eyes to blue wallpaper and feather pillows. 'Mmf.' I turned my head to see Loiter looking down at me, his brown eyes creased with worry.

'What happened?'

'You fainted. Demons aren't built for sunshine.' He held a cup out to me. 'Here, drink this.'

I obeyed. I felt like I'd lost a fight with a rabid tumble dryer. I tried to focus on him. 'Where am I? Where's everyone else?'

'We're in one of the bedrooms above the bar. It's Sarika's hotel. She's outside with Tommy, teaching her a few tricks.'

'We need to go—'

'You're not going anywhere for a few hours. Rest. We'll all still be here.' He nodded at a wooden dresser bearing a tray. 'Eat something, and take it easy. A few hours here or there won't make any difference.'

I was about to argue when my stomach rumbled loudly and I realised I was ravenous. I'd eaten nothing but stale cupcakes for days. 'OK.'

He got up. 'I'll be back to check on you in a couple of hours.'

He shut the door behind him, and I swung my legs out of bed and staggered over to the dresser. And wondered for a moment if I was seeing another mirage. Steak? I cut a mouthful and smiled. Real enough. Sarika really was the Bandit Queen. I took the tray over to a desk by the window and wolfed it all down.

Outside, I saw Tommy and Sarika in the garden at the back of the hotel, a heaped box of weapons between them. Tommy was grinning and waving a sword around, slashing the heads off a bed of spiky white plants as she backed away from Sarika, who was swinging an evil-looking machete. Great. Not only was I the wimp who'd fainted, but I was missing out on getting training from the one and only Bandit Queen. When I told this story in future I was so

leaving this part out.

I ate the rest of my food sulkily, watching them dart through the grass and parry and thrust. Then Tommy began teaching Sarika how to throw hira-shuriken. My eyes grew heavier and heavier as I watched, until I gave up and went back to bed.

Loiter woke me a few hours later with more food and drink. All my dizziness had vanished and after sleeping in a real bed for a few hours the heat of the desert felt like a distant memory.

Loiter peered at me.

'I feel better, honestly,' I said through a mouthful of pie.

'All right, if you say so. The girls are downstairs, finish that off and we'll go and join them.'

We found Sarika at a table in the saloon teaching Tommy the finer points of cheating at poker.

'Ladies,' said Loiter with a small bow.

Tommy leaped to her feet. 'Jinx! Are you OK? Loiter wouldn't let us disturb you.'

I smiled, trying to hide my embarrassment. 'I'm fine. Sunshine and demons don't mix, apparently.' I slid into a chair.

'Sarika's been teaching me to—'

There was a loud crash and thud and a dusty man

lurched through the saloon doors and fell at Sarika's feet. 'My queen, we have news of a rebellion!'

We all swivelled to stare at him.

'The train was passing and during our usual robbery I overheard the brutes...'

Sarika held up her hands. 'Abhay, calm yourself. I already know of this rebellion. I do not believe it will be in our interests, so I am helping my friends here to quell it. But please, tell us what you have learnt.'

Abhay got to his feet and bowed. 'My apologies, my queen. As you know, the train has been filled with all manner of heavy machinery in recent weeks...'

Loiter nodded. 'To try to crack the Wall open.'

Abhay seemed to finally realise there was a sloth standing next to Sarika and did a double take, but she placed a hand gently on his shoulder. 'Continue.'

'This time, however, the train was empty of equipment. There were only a few carriages of soldiers, and they seemed to be escorting a prisoner to The Ends.'

Sarika raised an eyebrow. 'A prisoner?' She turned to Loiter. 'Did you know about this?'

He shook his head and turned to Tommy and me. We both shrugged.

'Apparently not. I don't suppose you have any idea who

it is?' asked Loiter.

Abhay smiled proudly at being, after all, the bearer of newsworthy information. 'I can tell you exactly who it is, sir, for I overheard one brute call to another to guard him closely. The prisoner goes by the name Dantalion.'

My stomach lurched like the room had tipped sideways. I gripped the table. 'You're sure that was his name?'

'Yes, young sir.'

'Your brother?' said Tommy.

I nodded. Why would Astaroth kidnap my big brother? 'I don't understand, why...?'

Loiter looked like someone had spat in his margarita. 'That is not good news.'

We all turned to him.

He laid his paws on the table. 'When the Wall was originally built, it was locked in place with a keystone called the Sigil of Samael. Lucifer put it in place, and only he can remove it.'

'Or one of his bloodline, perhaps?' asked Sarika.

'Exactly,' said Loiter.

'Really? Hell's safety depends on some sacred Lego block?' said Tommy, a strange expression on her face. 'And without it, the Wall comes tumbling down?'

'But that doesn't make any sense,' I said. 'Morax caught

206

us when we were in Babel. If they need a D'Evil to remove the Sigil, why not take me?'

'Hmm,' said Loiter, 'that is strange. Perhaps you're still too young for it to work?'

'Or they didn't know about it till they read the book,' said Tommy. 'Remember? Morax marched off with the Nefarium and sent us straight to the Frozen Forest before he read it.'

I nodded. 'Of course. That's why they were looking for the Nefarium in the first place. They knew there was something in it about how to bring down the Wall. But they didn't know what.'

'But I don't quite understand,' said Tommy. 'Couldn't Lucifer just put this magical stone back in place when he finds out about it? Wouldn't the Wall go back to not being broken and that'd stop the war?'

Loiter shook his head. 'No, I don't think so. From what I remember, once the Sigil is removed, the Wall starts to crack apart pretty quickly. Maybe if he, or one of his descendants,' he nodded at me, 'got there in time, before the damage was too bad... But otherwise – goodbye, Wall, hello, war.'

Tommy and I looked at each other. 'No pressure, then,' I said.

Loiter clapped his paws together. 'There's no time to waste. And I'm pretty sure that's the first time I've ever said that. Jinx, I'm going to pop back to the palace and see if your father has returned. If not, I'll look for him on Earth. You two had better get on through the Caves of Wrath, and I'll try to join you as soon as I can, hopefully with your father and as many troops as we can muster.'

I nodded, still feeling sick about Dantalion. 'Loiter, we've got to rescue him.'

'And we shall. Now get going, and I'll meet you at the entrance to Nex. Try to stay out of trouble until then.' He turned to Sarika and bowed. 'Your Highness, I thank you for your hospitality.' He gave us a smile, and vanished into thin air.

Sarika stood up and we followed suit. 'Come with me to the arsenal, and I will see you are properly outfitted for your journey.'

That made me feel better. I grinned at the thought of wielding one of her killer machetes. Astaroth had better watch out, because I was coming for him, and I was taking no prisoners.

You Wouldn't Like Me
When I'm Angry

TOMMY BEAMED PROUDLY as she climbed into Doris's saddle, her satchel clinking with weapons.

I scowled at the tiny dagger strapped to my boot, which was the only thing Sarika had seen fit to arm me with.

'You can fly,' she'd pointed out. 'Tommy has no such powers. And weapons are dangerous in untrained hands.'

I picked up the reins with my stupid untrained hands and trotted off with the others out of Larceny. I glanced back at the peaceful, whitewashed town, half-wishing I was still in my feather bed. Then I remembered Dantalion and kicked my mount into a canter.

Night was falling by the time we came to what – judging by the requisite 'Abandon All Hope' sign – was the border between Thieves' Canyon and the Caves of Wrath.

Sarika frowned at us. 'Beware these caves. While you are

busy looking out for monsters, you may discover that the monsters are inside you. Farewell, my friends, I hope to see you again one day.' She nodded at me, smiled warmly at Tommy, and rode away.

'What does *that* mean?' I said, unnerved. 'The monsters are inside us? Like those flies that lay their eggs under your skin?'

Tommy wrinkled her nose. 'Ugh, gross, I hope not.' She watched Sarika ride into the distance and her face fell.

'Got a new heroine?' I said, nudging her.

'Are you telling me she's not cool? You are *not* telling me she's not cool.'

I thought of my lack of killer machete and sighed. 'Yeah, I guess so. Come on, then, let's go face these monsters.'

'Or, you know, avoid them.'

'That would work too.'

Before us, the canyons melted upwards into a soaring, yellow cliff face. There was no way up – the only route to the Nex Mountains and beyond was via a cave mouth that led underground, or through the railway tunnel for the Express. We'd already decided on the ride over that the narrow train tunnel would be a bad idea. We didn't exactly have a timetable, and neither of us had any desire to end up squished on the tracks.

I gazed up one last time at the roiling red sky. Loiter had promised the Caves wouldn't be dangerous – but he'd made no such claims about Nex. I crossed my fingers that he'd turn up by then.

We led Alfred and Doris down into the cave mouth, which soon became a tunnel smelling richly of clay. Torches lined the walls every few steps, lighting our way with flickering red light.

'I was expecting it to be dark and creepy,' said Tommy. 'This is a nice surprise.'

'Not really. Torches mean somebody lives here. I know Loiter said Tafrac was away, but then why are the lights still on? And if someone else is here, I'm guessing it isn't a sweet old lady with purring pets.'

'Gee, thanks for that. Let's hope the pets are toothless.'

'I wouldn't count on it.' I patted the dagger hidden beneath my trouser leg, suddenly glad to at least have some kind of weapon.

We wound up and down and round the caverns, the air warm and dry and tangy with earth. Occasionally we found ourselves at a fork, but the torches only ever led one way, so we followed them cautiously onwards, deeper and deeper underground. I fidgeted in my saddle, uncomfortable and restless. Why hadn't the rebels taken me? Had Morax really not yet known about the bloodline thing, or was there something wrong with me? Maybe I just wasn't evil enough to make the Sigil work.

Tommy started to sing, 'Hi ho, hi ho, it's off to work we go,' under her breath. It was really annoying.

'What's that song?'

'You know, from *Snow White* – the dwarves sing it when they're going underground to go mining.'

I shook my head. Stupid Earth stuff.

We plodded on further and further into the Caves. Apart from the neighing of the kravrons and the occasional scritch-scratch of a beetle, it was eerily quiet. Which made Tommy's singing stand out even more.

'Can you stop that?' I said, finally. 'You're like a homing beacon for monsters.'

'What monsters? We haven't seen a single living thing.'

'There are those beetles – they might just be biding their time till they swarm and attack and eat our eyeballs.'

She rolled her eyes. 'Don't be stupid, they're just beetles.'

'Oh, now you're an expert on Hell, are you, Bonehead?'

She yanked Doris to a stop and glared at me. 'Don't call me that! And judging by how much help you've been this whole trip, I reckon I know about as much as you do, palace boy. It's not like you've ever been out here either.'

'I...know things.'

'Like what? You were the one who wanted to ride the rabid carousel horses. *You* were the one who dragged us off to Babel and got us caught. *You* didn't remember we were in the Desert of Deception until it was almost too late.' She was practically spitting at me by now.

'Well, you were the one who ran off into quicksand like an idiot,' I lashed back. 'If I hadn't been there, you'd be history!'

Her face twisted into a mask of fury. 'If I'd known where I was in the first place, none of that would've happened! Everything that's gone wrong has been *your* fault. I should've listened when you told me you were unlucky.'

I opened my mouth to shout at her – and then I realised what was happening. I waved my hands frantically in front of me. 'Tommy, stop! It's the Caves of Wrath, they're infecting us, just like the Valley of Despair did. Just calm d—'

'I don't want to calm down! And I don't care! I should've known better than to make friends with a demon. All you want is to be evil. Well, where I come from, that's the *last* thing anybody wants. Humans want to be good! We don't always succeed, but we try.' She yanked her reins and sped off into the distance.

I cantered after her, swearing under my breath. Alfred gave me a worried look and I patted his leathery mane. 'It'll be OK, she'll get over it. It's these stupid caves.' But I was smarting over everything she'd said, my cheeks hot with anger. We came out of the tunnel and found ourselves in a huge cavern. Tommy was splashing across a shallow lake to the other side.

'Tommy, wait!' I bombed after her, but she ignored me. It was the last straw. How could she be so stupid? She knew it was the Caves' fault, and after them came Nex, we had to stay together or we'd never make it through alive. Worst of all, we were supposed to be friends. I splashed through the water until I was right behind her, leant forward, and grabbed Doris's tail to try to slow her down.

It didn't work out quite like I'd hoped. Doris kicked back at me, slipped, and fell over sideways, dragging Tommy down with her. Tommy landed in the water and let loose a stream of words I hadn't heard since the last time Dad lost at golf.

The kravron leapt nimbly to her feet, looking slightly disgruntled, as Tommy sat in the water coughing and spluttering. 'You – utter – *minion*!' she spat.

I clenched my fists, trying to contain the molten anger raging inside me. But there's no stopping a volcano. 'What were you thinking?' I yelled. 'We have to stay together, it's dangerous here! Why are you being so stupid?' The words tumbled out of my mouth in a spurt of fury. 'The whole of Hell is at stake, and my brother's life, and if you don't care about that you'd think you'd care about Earth, and how Astaroth is going to make things worse for every single human there if he gets into power!'

She shoved herself to her feet, dripping wet, her whole body shaking. 'I don't care about that! About any of that! You and your brother and your dad and the whole of Hell can...go to Hell, for all I care!'

A switch turned off inside me. My blazing anger melted away, replaced by cold, numb hatred. 'Whatever. I can save Hell and Dantalion by myself. I don't need some stupid, whiny, little dead girl to help me!'

Our eyes locked in mutual disgust.

'You are so pathetic,' she said coldly, wiping water out of her eyes. 'You think I was ever here to help you? Hah!' She swung up into her saddle. 'Did you really think I liked you? You, a demon? Not just a demon, but a whining, whimpering, useless demon?'

I rocked back like I'd been punched, but she didn't pause for breath.

'I went with you because I wanted to find out why I was

here, that was all! And see the city! Then I came with you on this ridiculous quest because—'

'Why? If you hate me so much, why *did* you come? You could've snuck back to the Fields of the Damned. Why—'

'Because of the Wall, you idiot! Did it never cross your thick brain what that means? There's a crack in the Wall – *a way out of here*. I only came with you so I could escape to Heaven!'

I gasped.

'And I don't need you to get through.' She sneered at me. 'What use are you? You'll just slow me down anyway.'

And she was gone, in a thudding of hooves and spray of ice-cold water.

MEANWHILE...

Lucifer was lying on a lilo in a pair of swimming trunks with little ducks on them, sipping a Piña Colada and trying to remember why he'd ever hated Earth so much. Persephone sat beside the swimming pool, her dark hair falling around her shoulders as she rubbed suntan lotion into her long brown legs. She kept looking up to smile at him.

There were no charming Greeks in sight. Well, not any more.

Best idea he'd ever had, popping in to see her for a surprise

visit for the first time ever. She knew how much he hated Earth, so he'd gained major points for 'putting up with' her charming Grecian villa for a few days. And he could thumb his nose at the Old Man at the same time. Like the Wall would ever really fall. He'd built it, hadn't he? It was impregnable. He'd check on it eventually. When he was good and ready.

He took another sip of coconut-y goodness. This is the life, he thought.

21

A Leap of Faith

SEVERAL LONG, SADDLE-SORE hours later, Alfred was getting restless and I was getting desperate for the light at the end of the tunnel. I hadn't found Tommy, but I wasn't really looking. Things had gone so wrong, I didn't know what either of us could say to make them right again. There were some things that could never be unsaid.

I knew now what Sarika had been talking about. 'The monsters inside you' hadn't been literal. We'd been the monsters all along.

I picked my way listlessly through the musty, torchlit tunnels and caverns, anger draining out of me with every step. Eventually, the raging fury that had burned so fiercely ebbed away, leaving only cold, black ashes of misery and exhaustion.

Just as I was about to doze off, I spotted daylight up ahead. Alfred's ears pricked up and he quickened his pace. Guess I wasn't the only one feeling claustrophobic. We came out onto a rocky plateau, and the pink sky above and fresh air in my lungs was such a relief, tears welled up in my eyes. I bent my head down on my saddle and sniffed loudly.

'Good to be outside, eh, buddy?'

Alfred whinnied in agreement.

I wiped my eyes and tried not to think about Tommy. The tears certainly weren't for *her*. She'd lied to me and betrayed me and blamed me and – and...the worst part of it was that she was probably right. I *had* got us chased by killer horses and woxes. I *had* got us caught in Babel. And I *had* been about as much use as a broken compass in Outer Hell. I'd messed up every step of the way, and I'd lost my only friend because of it.

'The problem with girls, you see, Alfred,' I joked, trying to cheer myself up, 'is they take everything so personally.'

He neighed brightly, but I could tell his heart wasn't in it.

'It was all the wrath demon speaking. She didn't mean to be so horrible.' But I wasn't sure if I believed it.

I slipped my aching body out of the saddle and led the kravron down the rocks. 'I don't even care if she wants to go to Heaven,' I went on. 'I mean, I'd rather she stayed, but I understand. I just don't know why she had to lie about it.'

He nudged me gently and I almost fell over. I was sloth-tired. I scanned the area for Loiter, but he was nowhere to be seen. There was nothing but a couple of miles of rocky plateau, broken only by the empty railroad track, leading up to the Nex Mountains, black and terrible against the sky.

What I needed was a good night's sleep. When I woke up, Loiter would be there, and everything wouldn't seem so bad. I pulled a blanket out of my saddlebag, curled up on a flat rock, and was out like a light.

When I woke, hours later, I could tell something was wrong. I lurched to my feet and scanned the sky for gamrins, but there was nothing there. *That.* That was what was wrong. There was still no one for miles except me and a softly snoring Alfred. Loiter should've been here by now. Where in Hell was he?

I pulled a sandwich out of my saddlebag and chewed it without tasting it, stalling for time. Anything might've happened to Loiter. Or to Dad. They might not be coming at all. For all I knew, Astaroth had locked them in the Unbreakable Cells, deep in the palace dungeons. But Dantalion was at the Ends, and Tommy was alone in Nex. I couldn't wait around any longer. I had to go and help them.

I shook Alfred awake and led him over the plateau towards the foothills of the dark, forbidding mountain range. Another train tunnel cut into the mountain, but I still didn't dare risk it. But how was I supposed to get through

Nex by myself? *A useless, whimpering demon*, Tommy had called me, and she was right. How was a skinny twelve-year-old supposed to fight off bands of crazed murderers, with nothing but a tiny dagger?

We trudged on, the peaks looming ever nearer, blocking out the light. I'd probably never see Tommy again, I realised. If she made it through Nex in one piece, and past the hellions at the Ends, that'd be it. She'd slip through the Wall and be gone forever. After everything we'd said to each other, maybe it was for the best. But the thought was like a rock in my stomach.

In the distance, I spotted a splintered wooden sign, and knew what it said before we even drew near. I stopped and scanned the area one last time for Loiter, but there was still no sign of him. Maybe he and Dad were marshalling the troops right that moment. Or perhaps he was still flitting all over Earth, trying to find Dad at his secret meeting. Either way, I couldn't waste any more time. I squared my shoulders. It wasn't about finding proof for Dad any more – it was about stepping up and solving the problem myself. It was time to be my father's son. I took a deep breath and thought, *What Would Lucifer Do?*

Not wait for his sloth bodyguard, that was for sure. And then a black shape appeared on the slope above me.

Tommy! I dropped Alfred's reins and scrambled up the slope towards her as fast as I could. But it wasn't her – it was a shivering, riderless Doris, and she didn't look happy. She slid down to the bottom of the slope and I caught her reins.

'What happened, Doris? Where's Tommy?'

As if she could tell me. And even if she could have, I had a sinking feeling the answer wouldn't have been cheering. Then I noticed something even worse. Tommy's bag of weapons hung, torn and filthy, from the saddle. So she was alone in the mountains, on foot and weaponless. Bad in so many ways. What had happened that had forced her to leave her weapons behind? I opened the bag but there were only a few hira-shuriken left, and they were no use to my untrained hands.

I stuffed them into my bag anyway, just in case, then jumped onto Alfred and pressed him up the slope, scree falling away beneath his hooves. He slipped and stumbled his way up as best he could, but I soon realised the mountain was going to be too steep for him. So maybe Tommy had let Doris go on purpose. But then why hadn't she taken her arsenal?

'I'm sorry, buddy, but this is where we say goodbye.' I slipped off the saddlebag and gave him a hug round the neck. 'You go home to Larceny with Doris.' I smacked him on the flank and he trotted back down the slope. At the bottom, he turned and whinnied at me, as if to say, 'Are you sure?'

'Go on, go home, I'll see you soon!' I yelled in as cheery a voice as I could muster.

He galloped off after Doris and I watched him go, heart sinking. No Alfred, no Loiter, no Dad, no Tommy. Mum far away on Earth. Even Bruce was back in Pandemonium. But I was a D'Evil, I could do this. I had to.

I scrambled up the slope and came to the top in less than an hour. I wiped the sweat off my brow and smiled. That hadn't been so hard. Then I saw the next peak. And it was far, far, higher. I sighed and trudged on through the slippery black scree.

I'd been dreading Nex infecting me like the Caves had done, but I felt no urge to start running around killing flummocks – the floppy-eared furballs which were the only life I'd seen so far. That was something, at least. But where were all the Nex Boneheads? I guessed it made sense that they didn't live on the steepest slopes. They probably had camps set up in the nooks and caves that littered the mountain range. I pushed on, worry for Loiter and Dantalion and Tommy whirring in my mind, but soon the climb took over, and all I could think was, *Left foot, right*

224

foot, grab that branch, pull yourself up, don't slip.

Several hours later, sweating and panting, I finally made it to the top of the second peak. It flattened out into a plateau, with grey, stunted trees poking up through the black earth like broken gravestones. More peaks spiked the sky to my right, but it was too misty to see what lay ahead. More mountains, knowing my luck. There was a loud crunch, and I jumped a mile. A flummock wagged its ears at me and bounded away. Great, now even fluffy animals scared me half to death. Some hero I was. At least I hadn't run into any murderers yet. Although the bad news was that there was still no sign of Tommy.

I stretched my aching arms and shoulders and decided to bed down for the night on a mattress of spine-tree needles. I hoped nothing would try to eat me while I slept.

I dreamed I was in Greece with Mum, in a whitewashed old villa. She was telling me how she'd be home soon, and I wouldn't have to go to Sharp Point, and everything was going to be OK. She went out onto a wide stone balcony and I followed her. The sun was setting and the skies and sea were lit up red, like I was home in Hell. Waves crashed on the shore and gulls cawed and dived. It was peaceful, and I was happy, and I wanted nothing more than to stay there forever...and then a blistering scream wrenched me awake, and I was back on the mountainside with the real red skies of Hell swirling above.

The scream – no, more of a war cry – echoed out again. *Tommy.* I fumbled to my feet, checked for my dagger, grabbed the saddlebag and took off through the scrubby trees. And almost fell to my death.

The plateau came to a sudden stop and I skidded to a halt. And stared. To my right, the brush melted into a fully formed forest, blocking my view. But straight ahead, I could see clearly – and there were no more mountains. No, instead the plateau dropped hundreds of sheer feet down, and in the distance was a pale, shimmering wall, rising so high up into the sky I couldn't see the top. It sparkled endlessly to the east and west, encircling Hell like a barbed-wire fence made of stars. The Infinite Wall. I held my breath at the sight.

It's one thing to know something exists, something incredible and awe-inspiring – but then to actually see it with your own two eyes – well, that's something completely different.

Tommy's voice rang out again and snapped me out of my daydream. This time I could make out words.

'Get away from me, you morons, or I'll slice you into little pieces!'

That was Tommy all right. But there was panic in her voice under the bravado. She needed help – and fast.

I dragged my eyes away from the glittering beauty of the Infinite Wall, threw my bag over my shoulder, and pelted into the woods to my right.

The dry forest of spindly spine trees scratched at me as I ran by. There was a strong scent of sap and of something else, something sharper. Blood. I sprinted harder. Shouts and taunts floated towards me from far away. I couldn't make out what they were saying, but it was obvious what had happened: Tommy had run into a band of killers, and they were after her. Somehow, I had to think of a way to rescue her.

'Argh!' A rough voice carried through the trees, followed by a thud.

She must've got one of them with a throwing star. So she still had some weapons left, that was a start. *Hang in there, Tommy*, I thought, *I'm coming. With my useless tiny dagger. No, don't think about that.*

She hates you, a voice at the back of my mind sneered as I tore through the wood, *why are you trying to save her? She thinks you're pathetic. You* are *pathetic.* I ignored it and rushed on, branches swiping at my clothes, feet slipping over loose dirt and rock. I spat out a mouthful of spine needles and all at once the trees were gone, and I was standing in a clearing. No, not a clearing – I'd gone right through the forest and out the other side.

I skidded to a stop, hot and out of breath, my chest heaving. A group of nine or ten brawny Boneheads stood yards away behind a large rock, whispering amongst themselves. They looked like the kind of men who stabbed first and asked questions later.

They hadn't noticed me. Yet. I threw myself into the dirt behind a bush. Now what? I peeked through the leaves, but the men hadn't moved. Before me the ground jutted out for forty or fifty yards until...nothing. It was a sheer drop. The Wall glimmered in the distance, while on the ground far below, tiny lights glowed from what had to be the traitors' camp.

Silhouetted on the very edge of the cliff stood Tommy. Her eyes were narrow and her jaw set, but I could tell she was terrified. She had a throwing star in one hand, and she was shouting, over and over. 'Don't you come any closer! I'll spike you, every last one of you!'

But without her bag, she only had six hira-shuriken. And who knew how many she'd already used. Then her voice cracked, and I knew at once – she'd thrown them all. The tiny piece of metal she was clutching was her last defence against a gang of bloodthirsty maniacs.

And soon *they* would realise that, too.

There was only one thing I could think of to do. I slipped off my coat and slid the saddlebag over my shoulder. I stole a glance at the men, but they were still too busy watching their prey to notice me. My heart was pounding so hard, I thought I might throw up. I took a deep breath, and pushed through the bushes.

Then I sprinted as fast as I could towards Tommy and hurled us both off the mountaintop into space.

22
Oh, Brother

THERE WAS A lot of screaming on the way down.

I could've sworn it was coming from Tommy, but it's possible I made a bit of noise too, especially when I saw how far away the ground was. For several panic-stricken seconds, I froze in terror, and we plummeted into nothingness like a stone, the wind whistling past my ears. Tommy clutched my neck so hard I could barely breathe. *Oh no, this wasn't the plan, squishy death was so not the plan, work, wings, work!*

The sheer mountainside flashed by, black and smooth as the walls of Darkangel Palace and my eyes watered with the speed of it, and this was it, we were going to die and there was nothing I could do about— no, that was it, the dream! All at once my dream of soaring over the palace came to me with ice-cold clarity, and a rush of calm descended on me. I could do it, I'd done it then, I could do it now. I unfurled my wings and swooped like a bat.

It took us both some time to regain our voices after we landed. Me, because I was too busy hearing triumphant trumpets playing in my head, proclaiming me the hero of all things, forever – and Tommy because she was panting and staring at me like I'd grown an extra head.

'Jinx!' she said at last. 'I've never been so glad to see anybody in my whole life.' She flung her arms round me and hugged me until I had to peel her off to avoid being crushed to death.

'Really?' I said. The triumphant trumpets were waning, and I was remembering everything she'd said in the Caves.

'Are you insane? You saved my neck. And you flew!'

'Not so pathetic, then?'

Her face fell. 'I'm so, so sorry for everything I said. I didn't mean any of it, you know that, right? You're my friend, I would never...' She trailed off, looking stricken.

I shuffled my feet back and forth, not knowing what to say. 'You were right, it was all my fault,' I said eventually. 'But why did you lie to me? I wouldn't have stopped you. I won't stop you. I understand, really.'

She twisted a plait round her finger, sheepish. 'I was going to tell you my plan as soon as we found the book. But then we got caught by Morax and I was angry with you for not telling me Lucifer was your dad. You lied too, Jinx. And that got us chucked in the Frozen Forest. Then by the time I'd got over that, we were friends and it felt too late to tell you the truth. And yes, I guess I did worry whether you'd try to stop me. Please don't be mad at me.'

I felt like a were-rhino had been lifted off my chest. I broke into a grin. 'It's OK, I'm not angry, I was just...' Hurt. I quickly changed the subject. 'Sorry if I scared you, I know how you're afraid of heights.'

She laughed. 'You know what, I think I might be cured. If I can survive jumping off a mountain, I can survive anything, right? But why are you alone – where's your sloth friend?'

My smile disappeared. 'I don't know. He never turned up.'

'Oh.'

'Yeah.' I looked around. We were in the foothills, but through the hillocks and rocks, I could see the lights of Astaroth's camp in the distance. The end of the line for the Infernal Express led off to my far left, but the train looked abandoned, for now at least. They'd clearly unloaded all their precious cargo. Including my brother.

'You think we should wait for Loiter, or...?'

I shook my head. 'He's already a whole day late. I...I'm scared they might have got him – and my dad.' Saying it out loud made me go cold inside.

Tommy sat on a rock and I sank down beside her. 'But if Loiter and Lucifer can do that magic zapping thing, surely they can't lock them up anywhere?'

'There is one place. The Unbreakable Cells in the palace dungeons. They were built especially to contain some of the older demons my dad fell out with. If Astaroth succeeds, he'll probably throw my whole family in there.' My eyes started to water and I rubbed them furiously.

'We're not going to let that happen.'

'We? I thought you were running off to the Other Side.' I squinted at her. 'I think you'd look better with horns than a halo, though.'

'I'll take that as a compliment.'

'Didn't mean it as one,' I deadpanned.

She smirked. 'I'm going to miss you, demon boy. But don't worry, I'm going to help you before I go. I always meant to do that, you know. And I really, really didn't mean any of those things I said. Forgiven?'

I nodded. 'Forgiven. So, what's the plan?'

'I was hoping you were going to tell me that.'

I puffed my cheeks out and stood up. 'OK, so...we don't have Loiter or my dad, but we do have a couple of advantages over the bad guys.'

'We have advantages over a huge demon army?'

'Yep. First of all, they don't know we're still alive, so we have the element of surprise. Second, I – I hope – can

233

activate the Sigil. So even if Dantalion's already taken it out of the Wall, I can put it back again. And lastly, Dantalion is pretty kickass. If we can rescue him, he can help us get away – and without either of us, Astaroth won't be able to break the Wall open again.'

'No broken Wall, no war with Heaven.'

'Exactly. It'll be way harder for Baal's army to take over if Hell isn't in chaos. And of course, my dad knows about all this now. Or at least, I hope he does.'

'I guess that's a start.'

I picked up the saddlebag and handed it to her. 'And this might help.'

She peered into it. 'My hira-shuriken! Yes!'

'Then again, maybe Loiter's in the dungeon and my dad doesn't know anything, still. Or *both* Loiter and my dad are in the dungeon...' I frowned. There were a lot of bad maybes. There was no point dwelling on them. 'Well, we'll worry about that when we come to it. Most of the demons back in Pandemonium will be on my dad's side. If they *are* locked up, we'll rally the troops and break them out somehow.'

'Alrighty, then. I like this new, positive you. Lead on, Captain Destiny.'

I led on, feeling better all the time. Everything was

going to be all right somehow, I just knew it. After all, if I could jump off the top of a mountain without ending up as strawberry jam, anything was possible. After an hour trudging through a barren, rocky landscape, we came to the edge of the camp. Tents, boxcars and heavy machinery were spread over an area the size of Larceny, and dozens of hellions milled about, looking bored. Astaroth had clearly been planning this for a long time. I wondered if all the soldiers were on his side, or whether they might not know the truth. If he'd lied to them and said this was something Dad had ordered, maybe I could get them to turn against him. The thought cheered me up even more.

We crawled up behind a low slope and lay on our bellies in the dirt. This close, the Infinite Wall hummed with energy, glittering and alive, like a billion firebugs threaded into a giant tapestry. It lit the camp like floodlights. Brown canvas tents, over a hundred of them, were laid out in neat lines to our right and left, with a wide empty space cutting through the middle in front of us. Alone in the centre stood a red velvet tent with gold tassels, three times the size of the others. Looking past it, I could see the heavy machinery – diggers, bulldozers and a grumpy were-rhino with a broken horn – standing idle by the Wall. Baal had clearly given up on conventional means of breaking the Wall. But now he had Dantalion, he didn't need to worry about that. I clenched my fists and scanned the area for my brother. Wherever he was, he was bound to be heavily guarded.

Tommy nudged me and nodded towards the red tent. 'Bet that's Baal's.'

But we didn't need to guess, because at that exact moment bull-headed Baal himself walked out of it, his hand on the shoulder of a tall, broad-shouldered demon.

'Who's that with him?' whispered Tommy.

'Dunno.' The other demon was facing away from me. A hellion, maybe? He didn't have an animal aspect. I shrugged. 'Another one of his minions, probably.'

Tommy made a mock-horrified face at me and I smirked.

Baal said something I couldn't hear, and several hellions snapped to attention and formed a phalanx around him and the other demon. They marched through the camp and came to a halt in front of the Infinite Wall. The soldiers stood to one side and one put a bugle to his lips and blew. And then the demon with Baal turned to him and nodded, and the Wall lit up his red face as clear as day. It was Dantalion.

'Is that...?' said Tommy.

I nodded grimly.

Dantalion put his hand to the Wall and a crack of

thunder split the air. They were too far away for us to see what was happening, but it was obvious. We'd arrived just in time to see Baal force my brother to remove the Sigil. I swore under my breath.

'We'll rescue him somehow,' said Tommy.

Dantalion pulled his hand away and another mighty crack echoed through the air and shook the ground beneath our feet. I watched in horror as a thick line began to zigzag up the shimmering face of the Wall. Baal, Dantalion and the hellions all took a few steps back and shielded their eyes. For a long moment, the Wall groaned like a waking giant – then a Hell-shattering screech rang out and a thousand shards of glowing debris flew out into the camp like a lightbulb exploding, leaving a blinding light streaming out of the gap.

'Heaven,' said Tommy, her voice hoarse with awe.

All I could think was, *If only I'd got here an hour earlier.* Who knew if the Sigil could even be replaced now? The hole was getting bigger all the time, it was already wider than Baal's tent.

'Look!' Tommy pointed away to our right. 'More cracks are appearing over there. Come on, we'd better hurry, before the whole thing shatters.'

But I barely heard her. I was staring straight ahead at

Dantalion. Because now he was walking back towards us –
and he was *smiling*.

I swallowed, not wanting to believe what I was seeing,
my mouth suddenly dry as dust.

Tommy nudged me. 'What's the matter? We can still fix
this, don't panic.'

I nodded at Baal and Dantalion, their heads bent together
like old friends. I felt like all the air had been sucked out of
my lungs.

'*Oh.*'

I couldn't even form that single syllable. The two of them smiled and chatted and I tried to pretend it wasn't happening, to wrap myself up in denial like a cosy blanket. But it didn't work. There it was, staring me right in the face. He'd never been a prisoner at all. The hellions on the train hadn't been guarding him – they'd been *protecting* him. He'd been the ringleader all along, not Astaroth. So much for everything being all right.

My own brother had betrayed us.

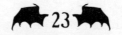 23

Just Another Brick in the Wall

I SHOOK MY head. 'I...I always looked up to him, you know? He was so good at being evil. I wanted to be just like him.'

'Guess he's a bit too good at being evil if he's betrayed your dad. So it was never Astaroth at all. Wow.'

My mouth tasted like ashes. I thought of how Dantalion had got revenge on Benny and Arael for me just a few days ago. My perfect big brother. So much for that.

Tommy nudged me. 'See, maybe you aren't such a failure as a demon after all. There are worse things than making a few mistakes. Looks like being evil isn't as great as you thought.'

I didn't know what to say. I felt numb.

'Look, don't panic. You can still undo what Dantalion's done, it isn't too late. We still have the element of surpri—'

We were lifted clean off our feet by two giant hellions.

Tommy kicked and flailed but I was still too shell-

240

shocked to put up much of a fight. They yanked our hands behind our backs, tied them roughly together, and marched us into the camp.

'Looks like we'll be getting a closer look at the red tent, then,' muttered Tommy.

By the time we got there, Baal and Dantalion had wandered off, and instead we found Morax, sitting at a desk reading some papers, black fur gleaming in the light.

'Found these two snooping about, Duke,' said the hellion behind me. 'What you want done with 'em?'

Morax didn't even raise his head. 'Kill them.'

Oh, hellfire. 'Wait, I...I'm Dantalion's brother, you have to let me speak to him!' I said desperately.

Morax, to my immense relief, looked up. 'You? You're supposed to be dead.' My relief wilted beneath his icy stare. He tapped his claws on the desk and growled. 'Torrus, go and fetch Mr D'Evil, would you? See if he wants this brat alive. Mal, search them then throw them in the backroom.'

'Yes, sir.'

The hellion called Mal took Tommy's saddlebag, patted us down then shoved us into another room at the back of the huge tent, which turned out to be a bedroom, complete with four-poster bed. Morax clearly liked to travel in style. But on the way, we passed a third room, where I saw something that almost made my eyes pop out. It was a polished wooden table – and sitting in the middle was a carved, hexagonal stone.

Mal tied us firmly to a bedpost each, then left us alone, half-sitting on the floor, our hands raised uncomfortably behind our backs. It was stupid, but I was almost glad we'd been caught so I could yell and scream at Dantalion for being a verminous traitor. Which is exactly what I did when he walked into the room five minutes later.

'How could you? We're your family, how can you betray us for those stupid traitors out there? Dad believed in you, *I* believed in you, Dantalion!'

He shook his head and sighed. 'I'm sorry, bro. But there's no point whining now, it'll all be over soon. I'll be the new King of Hell, and nobody'll object too much because I'm Lucifer's son. Not to mention the fact that I'll have all of Baal's armies behind me.'

'What about Dad? How could you do this to him?'

'Dad'll be in the old folks' home, where he belongs. Otherwise known as the Unbreakable Cells.'

I swore at him some more.

'Insulting me isn't going to help, Jinx.'

'No, but it makes me feel better.'

'This family reunion is charming,' said Morax, 'but what

do you want me to do with them?'

Dantalion pursed his lips, and there was a slight flicker in his eye. 'Don't kill them, they might come in useful as hostages. When this is all over, they can go in the Cells with everyone else.'

'How gracious of you,' I spat.

He shook his head and left the room with Morax.

I was so furious I felt like I was back in the Caves. I glared daggers at his receding back until a soldier pulled down the flap and left us alone in the bedroom. I closed my eyes and took a deep breath. I'd lied to Dantalion, yelling at him hadn't made me feel any better. It'd take more than that to cheer me up after finding out my brother was a traitor. And now we were captured and alone without back up, and the Wall was cracking open with every passing second. It was a disaster.

'Another fine mess you've got me into,' said Tommy.

'Really?' I said. 'You're going to start blaming me aga—' I noticed her lip curl. 'Why are you smiling?'

She nodded at my foot. 'Seems they forgot to search you properly.'

I looked down and saw the tiny dagger Sarika had given me, poking out from under my trouser leg. I'd completely forgotten about it. Tommy was right. Sarika *was* cool.

Several minutes' painful contortion later, I'd managed to pull the knife out of its sheath. I sawed clumsily away at the ropes behind me.

'So the bad news is Dantalion really is a supervillain,' I said. 'But the good news is the Sigil's in the next room.'

'What? Are you sure? How do you even know what it looks like?'

'Well, it might be another important, ancient-looking stone, but I doubt it.' I gave one last yank and my ropes fell away. I untied Tommy as quickly as I could.

Another almighty crack split the air, and the ground heaved beneath my feet. I hung on to the bedpost until it died down.

'Sounds like you better put it back quick,' she said. 'Or there won't be any Wall left.'

I peeked through the flap into the main room and saw Morax scurry outside. Two hellions stood guard outside the main exit, but there was no one left inside. 'Come on.'

We slipped into the next room.

Tommy laid her hand on the stone. 'Amazing something so small can cause so much trouble.'

'Never stopped you,' I said with a smirk. I studied the Sigil. Would it work for me, or was I not evil enough? There was only one way to find out. I picked it up.

And…nothing happened.

I could've cried.

'Oh look, my bag!' said Tommy. She stuffed some throwing stars into her pockets.

I just stared miserably at the rock in my hands. But then slowly, ever so slowly, it began to glow. Faintly at first – then brighter and brighter, a soft red. 'Phew.'

'What? You didn't think it'd work for you?'

'Thought did cross my mind.'

It was disproportionately heavy for something the size of a dinner plate, and for a terrifying moment, I almost dropped it. I cradled it in my arms and scooted to the back of the tent, where Tommy was already making a slit in the velvet with my dagger. We stuck our heads through and peered outside.

'Wish I had shades,' she said.

'You're not wrong.' It was daytime now, and with the light from the Wall, every inch of the camp was lit up like a football stadium.

She raised an eyebrow. 'This is not exactly helpful for sneaking around.'

I slunk round the side of the tent and peeked out. Almost everyone in the camp was gathered by the ever-growing gap in the Wall. 'There's no way we can put it back where

245

it came from.'

'No, but I saw cracks further along too.' She pointed through the tents to our right. 'Along there. And they're all distracted right now. Come on – we might not get another chance! They'll notice we've gone soon.'

We slipped cautiously through the tents, but most of the hellions had disappeared off to look at the spectacle of the disintegrating Wall. The minute we reached the edge of the camp, I broke into a run. I clambered over a large rock and hunkered down behind it, puffing like a freight train. We weren't safe, but we were out of sight for now.

I turned to Tommy. 'OK, so where are these other gaps?'

She pointed to my right. 'Over there, see, two of them. Let's hope you don't have to put the Sigil back in the same place it was originally.'

'Yeah.' If that was the case, we had no hope. I peered over the rock at the camp, but there were no hellions nearby. I scrambled to my feet. 'Here goes nothing.'

We jogged along the rocky ground until we came to the first crack. It was about as wide as me. A few yards away was another hole, barely big enough for a bat to fly through. That was the one.

'So...' she said.

I suddenly remembered what came next. I bit my lip and

turned to face her.

She twisted a plait around her finger and toed at the ground. 'So. I guess this is goodbye, then.'

I tried to smile. 'Enjoy the Other Side. If you ever get bored of all those do-gooders, you can always come back. We won't hold it against you.'

But it was a lie, and we both knew it. Once I replaced the Sigil, the Wall would close forever, and there would be no turning back.

She gave me an awkward hug, the heavy stone between us. 'Thanks for saving my life and everything. Or, you know, my afterlife.'

'Ditto.'

'I hope everything works out for you and your dad. Give Bruce a hug from me.'

'I will.'

She put her hand on the Wall, next to the gap. The light glowed right through it, turning it red. 'Right, here we go.'

'Right.' I swallowed. If anyone ever tells you goodbyes are easy, they're lying.

'Tommy, I...'

'Me too. Go save the universe, Captain Destiny.' She smiled crookedly, stepped into the light, and vanished.

I stared after her for a second, but the light was too

bright to see past. I suddenly felt very small and very alone. She was really gone. After everything we'd been through together, she was just...*gone*.

I hefted the Sigil up in my arms and shivered. A strong wind had started to blow and the sky was rumbling like a storm was coming. Well, that wasn't wrong. I bit my lip hard. I could be sad about Tommy later. Right now I had Hell to save.

I ran over to the smaller hole, crossed my fingers, and held up the Sigil. Then I pressed it into the glowing gap and waited.

And stared.

And waited some more.

Nothing happened.

Until it did.

The Wall spat the Sigil out like a cherry stone.

Oh, hellfire. That was so not part of the plan.

Luckily, it didn't break. I picked it up and glared at it. Would it work if it was put back in its original spot? Or had it lost its power? Was the Infinite Wall irretrievably damaged forever?

I shielded my eyes from the dazzling light and looked back towards the camp. There was only one way to find out.

I Do Something Totally Unhinged

I DASHED BACK through the camp until I came to the final row of tents before the central clearing. The storm was gaining pace, although there was still no rain. Between the ominous cracks and mini-earthquakes coming from the Wall, and the distant rumbling in the sky, it felt like Very Bad Things were about to happen. I just hoped they wouldn't happen to me.

I slipped into an empty hellions' tent and peered through the flap at where Dantalion, Baal, Morax and several hundred hellions were milling about, gazing up at the crack in the Wall, which was already the size of a house. *Minions.* How was I supposed to put the Sigil back when they were all watching? Not to mention replacing it when there was nothing there but thin air. I sighed. Tommy would've had some brainwave, if only she'd been here.

The rumbling of the storm – or was it the Wall? I couldn't tell any more – grew louder and louder. In the distance, high up in the sky, thick black clouds were approaching. No, thick *red* clouds. Thick red clouds that were travelling faster than any hurricane I'd ever seen. Baal shouted and pointed at the sky.

And then all Hell broke loose.

The clouds parted into a thousand tiny dots and all at once the sky was filled with the beating of wings and the roar of war-cries. And in the midst of it, larger than life, soared Dad, with an expression on his face that said *I will murder every last one of you. To death.*

I'd never been so glad to see him in all my life. Baal and Dantalion spewed orders at the rebel army, but already half of them had run off in all directions. Unfortunately, the other half looked like they were ready to stand and fight. Of course, standing was all they could do, since they had no wings. Where had Dad found soldiers who could fly? Then I spotted Morgana and Zethar and understood – Dad had rounded up the whole family. Dantalion might've sold out, but they hadn't. My brothers and sisters descended like a flaming forest fire, and in seconds the whole camp rang with the sounds of battle.

Baal and Dantalion plunged right into the fray, but Morax took one look at six hundred angry D'Evils and scarpered straight towards the tents. Towards *me*. I jumped to one side a second before he pushed through the flap, his face panicked.

Serves you right, I thought. I lifted the Sigil up as high as I could and smacked him on the back of the head. He slid to the ground, out cold.

'Hah! That's for chucking us in the Frozen Forest!' I crowed. I'd like to say I didn't do a little victory jig. So let's just say I didn't.

I shoved the Sigil under my shirt and pulled back the tent flap. A few soldiers were fighting near the Wall, but most of them had spread out through the camp. I gulped. Time to be a hero. It was now or never. I bolted out of the tent and nearly had my head cut clean off by a hellion with a machete. I ducked and sped on over the dusty ground, clutching the stone to my stomach. Flames blasted left and right and metal screeched on metal all around me. I weaved through the battle, for once glad to be a puny twelve-year-old – no one seemed to be interested in trying to fight me. They probably thought I wasn't worth the effort. We'd see about that.

A hellion in front of the Wall went up in a burst of flame and ran off screaming. I hurtled past, nose twitching at the stench of smoke, and skidded to a stop in front of the huge gap in the Wall. The dazzling light burned my eyes, but I ignored the pain and fumbled the Sigil out from under my shirt. *Please work*, I thought, *please, please...*

I held it up in front of me – then there was a whoosh of wings and I was knocked off my feet. The sigil skittered across the dirt out of reach. I cupped my hands over my eyes and saw Dantalion himself looming over me.

'You! You've ruined everything,' he shrieked, his usually calm voice like nails down a blackboard.

I grabbed for my dagger but Dantalion stamped on my hand with a crunch of bones, making me yelp. He ignored me, kicking the dagger away. His face twisted with rage and he flexed his black wings furiously, casting a shadow on the tent wall behind him.

'You little idiot, this is all your fault, isn't it? *You* told Dad about my plans. Do you realise what you've done? The whole empire is a shadow of its former self. Humans are running free to do what they please! Soon the word 'evil' will be nothing but a memory on Earth!'

'He's a hero and you're a traitor,' I yelled, 'and Hell's fine as it is!'

His dark eyes glowed feverishly as he took another step back. He raised his hands and sparks flew from them. 'Say goodbye to your beloved Hell, little brother, because this is the last you'll see of it!'

I tensed, ready to be turned to ash – and then a tiny bat swooped down out of the smoke and sank its fangs into his cheek.

'Aughh!' Dantalion flapped at Bruce, changing in an instant from Terrifying Arch-Nemesis to Little Kid Dancing Around Dodging a Bee.

I grinned. Never let anyone tell you a vampire bat isn't a useful pet. I scrambled to my feet and grabbed the Sigil, just as Dantalion managed to unhook Bruce's teeth and fling him into the air. He turned to face me, blood dripping from his chin, fury emanating from every pore.

And then I had a totally unhinged idea. A hinged idea would've been better, but I didn't have time to think, since I was facing a vengeful supervillain who was about to burn me to a crisp.

'You're right,' I blurted, taking a step back, 'it *is* all my fault. Can't imagine how embarrassing it must be to lose a war to your twelve-year-old brother. Bet your friends would never let you hear the end of it.' I grinned crazily at him.

Dantalion hissed like a snake and raised his hands once more.

'But if you want me dead, you're going to have to catch me first!' And I spun round and dived through the Wall into Heaven.

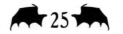

25

Evilly Ever After

A JOLT LIKE a thousand volts of static electricity zapped my bones, and blinding light filled my skull. I opened my mouth to scream—

And landed gently on a soft carpet of grass.

I shook my head and lay panting on the ground. Still alive. That was nice. I raised myself onto my hands – I didn't feel any weaker. Maybe being a rubbish demon was good for something, after all. It wasn't like I had a lot of evil for Heaven to drain. I looked up and...saw that I was surrounded by feet. *Oops*.

I was in a meadow, an old oak tree before me, blue skies shimmering above, and an atmosphere of utter peace broken only by the squadron of angels glaring down at me like I'd gatecrashed their garden party. *Heaven*. Wow. I'd certainly never expected to see this place in my lifetime.

'Don't move!' said an angel who looked like the captain, pointing a flaming sword at me. Her black face was smooth as marble and as perfectly carved, and her huge white wings shimmered with light.

I glanced back at the Wall, but there was no sign of Dantalion. *Yet.* I had a feeling he wouldn't give up on revenge that easily.

'Doesn't make any sense,' muttered a blonde angel next to the captain, shaking his head. I noticed now that a crowd of humans was gathered behind the angels, peering over their shoulders curiously. 'Where's the demon horde? Why would they send a small boy?'

Then I heard a familiar voice.

'Jinx? Jinx!'

Before the cordon of angels could stop her, Tommy skidded to a stop in front of me. 'Don't hurt him! He isn't evil!'

The angels looked more confused than ever.

I smiled at her. 'Thought you'd be long gone by now.'

She shrugged. 'Might've been keeping an eye on how you were doing. And since the Wall is still broken, you didn't seem to be doing too well. Heaven doesn't seem much safer right now, to be honest.'

As if to prove her words, there was a crash and a fizz and Dantalion appeared through the Wall. The angels took a few steps back, swords outstretched. I grabbed Tommy's arm and whispered in her ear. She nodded and we backed away slowly.

My big brother took no notice of the angels and their swords. He was too focused on getting revenge. 'Thought I wouldn't come after you, eh, Jinx?' he said with a sneer. 'Thought you could just run away and hide like a coward?'

I backed away further, and he strode towards me until he was standing beneath the oak tree. I held my hands up. 'Yup, you've got me, how silly of—'

Two things happened at once.

Dantalion raised his hands and fired – and Tommy hurled a handful of throwing stars. But nothing but a few sparks came from Dantalion's fingertips – and now his wings were impaled against the tree trunk by four hira-shuriken.

He glared at his hands like they'd betrayed him. 'Why...why didn't...'

'I knew your fire wouldn't work here,' I said, although *fervently hoped* would've been more accurate. 'Dad once admitted to me that demons have no power in Heaven. But you were so keen to start a war you didn't bother to look into that piece of lore, did you?'

Dantalion tugged at his wings, raging. 'We never planned to start a war, you idiot! That was just an excuse so Baal would be put in charge of all the troops, and then we could take over. But one way or another, I'll get out of here soon, and then you'll both be very, very sorry!'

'Oh, but I don't think we will,' I said. 'You see, judging by the angelic guard, God was worried about his subjects getting infected by Evil seeping through from Hell.' I turned to the angel with the flaming sword. 'Isn't that right?'

The angel captain nodded, still frowning like she was trying to figure out a really hard crossword clue. 'That's right. But I don't understand, demon – whose side are you on?'

'The side of no one getting hurt.' I turned back to Dantalion. 'Did you think it only worked one way? It

doesn't. Every second longer you spend here, the more you'll be infected by Goodness. We learnt all about it at school. In a few days, you'll be as gentle as a puppy.'

Dantalion's eyes grew wide. He yanked harder at his wings, but they held fast. 'You can't do this!' he screeched. 'It's...it's undemonlike! Dad will be furious!'

I smirked. 'Furious that I've neutralised his traitorous son? I doubt it.'

Tommy ran over to the captain, and she lowered her sword. 'Please, Jinx is telling the truth, he just wants to prevent a war.' She pointed at Dantalion. '*He's* the bad guy. He started this whole thing! You need to lock him up.'

Tommy waved at me again. 'Plus, he's the only one who can close the Wall. You have to let him go.'

The captain pointed at the Sigil. 'What is that?'

'Our only chance to prevent a war,' I said. 'It'll close the Wall once I replace it. Please, let me go and I promise you'll never see me again.'

A furious shriek came from behind us and we all turned to look at Dantalion. He was thrashing against the tree, his eyes like daggers, hurling obscenities at the angels surrounding him. The captain shook her head at me.

'I'm sorry, but I can't trust you. You're a *demon*. I'm going to have to take you into custody. Both you and the sweary one over there are going straight to Purgatory. For good.'

'Wait!' Tommy put her hand on the angel's arm. 'You trust me, right?'

She looked down at her. 'I suppose so.'

'So. Let me go back with him and make sure he closes the Wall.'

The captain looked at Tommy, then at me, then over at Dantalion. She pinched the bridge of her nose like she was beginning to get a migraine. 'I hate Mondays.'

'OK?' said Tommy.

The captain sighed. 'Do you understand what you're saying? You're willing to leave Heaven?'

'Yes,' said Tommy, her voice coming out really small.

The captain nodded, her face stern. 'OK. If I let the demon boy go alone I can't be sure he'll replace this Sigil. But if you agree to go back with him, then he's free to leave.'

I grabbed her arm. 'Tommy, you can't...'

'I have to, or the Wall will never close. It's the only way to keep everyone safe.'

'No!' I couldn't bear to be the reason Tommy didn't get to stay in Heaven after all. I took a step towards the Wall but before I could blink, the captain had her blade pointed at my throat.

'Son of Lucifer, either your companion goes with you, or

I'll have no choice but to lock you away in Purgatory with this Dantalion character. Despite your protestations, you may yet be on his side. For all I know, you're planning to return with an armed horde. I'm sorry, but I'm afraid I just can't trust a demon's word.'

Tommy put her hand on my shoulder. 'It's OK, Jinx. Honestly. Come on, we've got a Wall to close.' She took one last look back at Heaven, as though she were trying to fix it in her mind, then dragged me away from the angels.

'You know you won't be able to come back, don't you?' I said.

'I know.'

I bit my lip and nodded.

We walked towards the Wall, sparing a glance at Dantalion as we passed. The angels were prising him away from the tree and encircling him in some kind of fiery bonds.

'Are you sure it's safe to leave him here?' asked Tommy.

I looked at the brother I had once so wanted to be like. Already the anger had begun to die out from his eyes. Goodness was infecting him. 'I hope so.'

I took a deep breath, prepared myself for more pain, and leaped back through the gap in the Wall, Tommy beside me. But to my relief, I didn't get electrocuted this time. I supposed I was going through the right way. The red skies of Hell on the other side were the prettiest thing I'd ever seen. I resisted a strong urge to kiss the ground and scanned the camp. The battle had petered out to a few fights here and there.

A squawking bat fluttered down onto my shoulder. 'Thanks for the distraction earlier,' I said, stroking his wings.

Tommy nudged me. 'Come on, then.'

I spun round, and, feeling slightly silly, pushed the Sigil forward into the empty, shimmering gap. Despite what I'd said to the angel, I wasn't holding out much hope that it would work. It had already failed once.

For a moment, nothing happened. I took my hands away, waiting for the Wall to spit the stone out again. But it didn't. It hovered magically in thin air, and I wondered if there were some magic words I was supposed to say or something. Then there was a gigantic whooshing noise, like a thousand birds diving through the air – and all at once the Wall was whole again.

I stared at Tommy, open-mouthed, then back at the Wall. It was like nothing had happened. No cracks, no holes, nothing but a pale shimmering tapestry of tightly knitted stars as far as the eye could see. A great clamour erupted behind me and I spun round to see all my brothers and sisters hollering and cheering.

The battle was over. We had won.

There was a loud beating of wings and Dad dropped to the ground in front of me. For a moment, he just stared: first at me, then at the Wall, then at Tommy, then back at me. Then he marched over, picked me right up off the ground and gave me a bone-crushing hug.

'You...I...well...' I stuttered.

He put me down and took me by the shoulders. 'Jinx, I've never been so proud of any of my children. You're a

chip off the old block.'

It took me several seconds to pick my jaw off the ground. 'I'm sorry I ran away,' I blurted out.

He waved his hand dismissively. 'Don't be ridiculous! First bad thing you've ever done! Made me smile. And I'm sorry I gave you such a hard time about being Good. It's not such a surprise, really, when you're only half demon. Can't be blamed for having a bit of your lovely mother in you.'

My head spun. 'That's all it was? Mum? I thought I was some kind of freak.'

He chuckled. 'Nothing wrong with being a freak. If no one was ever different, everything would always stay the same, and that'd be pretty boring, wouldn't it? Nothing would ever evolve. If your old man hadn't been a bit of a freak, Hell wouldn't even exist. Imagine that!'

I'd never thought of it like that before. 'I'm very glad Hell exists,' I said.

'Me too. Anyway, now...' He nodded at the Wall. 'Well, you'll forever be remembered as the demon who saved the realm.'

I grinned so hard I thought my face would split.

He squinted. 'But where's Dantalion?'

I pointed at the Wall. 'In Heaven, busy being infected by Goodness. I don't think you need to worry about him any more.'

Dad's eyebrows shot up. 'That...is evilly clever,' he said. 'Well done. And who's this?' He nodded at Tommy.

'Dad, don't be mad, I know she's a Bonehead, but I couldn't have done any of this without her. She saved my life twice!'

He raised an eyebrow. 'Did she now?'

'And she fed her nasty uncle to a circus lion!'

He burst out laughing. 'Well, in that case she can stay. Might be a bad influence on you.' He stopped laughing and stared at Tommy for a moment. 'Hang on, though, how old are you?'

'Eleven.'

'Then you shouldn't be here.'

'That's what everyone keeps telling me.'

'I checked at Babel,' I said. 'They thought it was a mistake. There's no record of her.'

Dad's eyes glowered red. 'A mistake? There are no mistakes in Hell.'

Tommy shrugged. 'I don't mind, really. Jinx was right. Halos don't suit me.'

'Well, someone's due a toasting down in administration, but if you're sure.'

'I am.'

I put my arm round her. 'Seriously, are you OK? I'm so

sorry you had to leave Heaven.'

She poked me in the ribs. 'Pfft, where was I going to find a friend in Heaven as annoying as you?'

I grinned. 'It'd be hard.' I suddenly remembered something. 'Dad, where's Loiter, is he all right?'

'He's fine. I asked him to stay back at the palace to keep an eye on things while I was gone. It took him almost two days to find me on Earth, so he was pretty exhausted by the time we got back. I came as soon as I heard.'

'Just in time.'

Dad frowned. If I hadn't known him better, I would've sworn he looked...sheepish. *Really* sheepish. 'Yes. I decided to pop in and see your mother. Couldn't have chosen a worse time for it. I'm sorry if I let you down, Jinx.'

I didn't know what to say. Usually this conversation was the other way round. 'I'm just glad you're here. Except...I don't suppose there's any chance you've changed your mind about Sharp Point?'

He quirked an eyebrow. 'Considering you've just quashed the biggest rebellion in Hell's history, I doubt there's much left for them to teach you.'

I exhaled. It wasn't remotely true, but I wasn't going to tell him that. I gestured at the smoking ruins of the camp. 'So now what?'

'Now we clear up this mess, improve security here at the Wall, lock a few demons away in a nice, deep dungeon, and put our feet up and have a banana milk.'

I did a double-take. 'Banana milk?'

He headed off back through the camp, and Tommy and I hurried after him. 'You think I don't know what my youngest son's favourite drink is?'

No. No, I hadn't. 'Do I get my bust in the hall outside your study now, with all the other illustrious demons?' I joked.

'Careful. Pride comes before a fall, you know,' he said with a smirk.

An evil thought – possibly my first ever – came to me. 'Mum doesn't know about all this, does she? The Wall breaking, the rebellion, *her beloved son almost getting killed multiple times.*'

Dad skidded to a halt.

I looked up at him innocently.

He shook his head in impressed disbelief. 'One marble bust of Jinx D'Evil, coming right up.'

Epilogue: Tommy

THERE WAS A knock at the door.

Not just any knock: an *important-sounding* knock.

I spun round from my new bedroom window. I'd just got here, was I in trouble already? I took a deep breath and yanked the door open quickly to get the pain over with.

A wizened grey demon stood outside, spindly wings fluttering like he'd arrived in a hurry. He fixed me with glowing red eyes. 'Lucifer, Prince of Darkness, Enemy of Righteousness, Lord of the Flies, summons you. Follow me and I shall take you to my master. Refuse, and the consequences—'

'Yes, yes, I get it,' I interrupted. 'You could just say Jinx's dad wants to see me.'

The messenger demon blinked at me. There was an awkward silence. 'Do you refuse to follow me, Tomasina Covelli?' he said finally.

'Don't be silly, of course not.'

I stuck my hands in my pockets and marched off to meet the Devil.

After following the messenger demon down two flights of stairs and through about fourteen creepy-looking passageways, we came to a halt in front of a pair of vast black doors carved with all kinds of Hellish goblins and eerie thingummies. Which were moving. Why did everything in Hell have to *move*? The demon knocked on the door and gestured for me to enter.

Lucifer's study was like the prettiest mini-library ever. All the walls were lined with bookcases, with the odd painting in between, and one wall with leaded windows overlooking Pandemonium. In the middle stood a mahogany desk big enough to sleep on, and behind the desk sat a thoughtful-looking King of Hell.

'Hello, Your Majesty,' I said.

He nodded at me. 'Hello, Tommy. Please, sit down.'

Oh crikey. I was so in trouble. I was going to survive flesh-eating carousel horses and two-headed vultures and bottomless libraries all to get squished like a fly by Jinx's dad. I clenched my fists. 'It's not fair—' I started to say, but I stopped in disbelief.

Lucifer had waved his hand, and in an instant a transparent, floating computer screen had appeared above his desk. 'I told you I don't like mysteries or mistakes,' he said. 'So I searched my files.'

'You...you have computer files?' I said, dumbfounded. 'But what about all the little cabinets in the library—'

'Oh those. They're for Bonehead trivia. You don't think I wouldn't have the important stuff backed up, do you? I'm not stupid. One tiny fire and I might lose track of a thousand souls owed. No, no, no.'

'Souls owed?' I said, getting more confused by the minute.

Lucifer waved at himself. 'Hello, Devil, people sell their souls to me?'

'Oh. Right. Yes.'

'And I think I might have found the secret behind your, er, surprise visit.'

Surprise visit. That was one way of putting it.

He flicked his finger in the air and a wall of text streamed past. It stopped on what looked like a passport page, complete with photo.

I gasped. Floating in front of me was a large picture of my Uncle Boozy, the ringmaster.

'So that's it,' I said glumly. 'I am meant to be here. For killing him.'

'Look closer,' said Lucifer.

I looked. And looked again. Stamped across the passport in big red lettering were the words SOUL COLLECTED.

'He...he sold his soul to you? Boozy?' I said, my mind spinning.

'He did. I remember him now. Nasty, sweaty man. Greedy. Wanted to make lots of money. So I told him I'd make his grubby collection of tents one of the most successful travelling circuses in the world, in exchange for his soul. And as you can see, he couldn't sign fast enough.'

'But...but the circus wasn't even that good,' I said, bewildered. 'I mean, it did OK—'

Lucifer smirked. 'Well, I did say *one of* the most successful circuses in the world. The fifty-ninth, to be precise.'

I burst out laughing. 'I like you.'

He looked immeasurably pleased. 'Thank you, my dear, the feeling is mutual. Now, when a Sold Soul is sent to Hell upon death, there's a strong force field around it. Can't let any of the blighters escape, you see. So, I can't say for certain, because as far as I know it's never happened before, but I think you might've just been in the wrong place at the wrong time.'

'And been sucked down to Hell with him?'

'Exactly.'

'So it's not my fault? I'm not the most evil kid ever?'

He flicked his wrist and the transparent screen disappeared, along with Boozy's ugly face. 'No.' He grinned. 'But I daresay there's time to fix that yet.'

So it had been my uncle's fault all along, not mine. A

huge weight I hadn't even known I was carrying slid off my shoulders. 'Thank you, Your Badness. Thank you so, so much.'

Lucifer inclined his head in a short bow. 'Welcome to Hell, young lady. I think you're going to like it here.'

There was a sentence I never thought I'd hear. I looked out of the window at the soft amber mist and curling red towers of Pandemonium. It was really quite breathtakingly beautiful. I grinned back at the Devil. 'I think I'm going to like it here too.'